Hidden

(Amish Secret Widows' Society Book 2)

Samantha Price

Copyright 2014 Samantha Price
All Rights Reserved

ISBN 978-1502847515

This book is a work of fiction. Any resemblance to any person, living or dead, is purely coincidental. The personal names have been invented by the author, and any likeness to the name of any person, living or dead, is purely coincidental.

Chapter 1

But without faith it is impossible to please him: for he that cometh to God must believe that he is, and that he is a rewarder of them that diligently seek him.
Hebrews 11:6

Emma sniffed the air; it smelled as though the chocolate chip cookies she was baking were ready. She had burned the first batch that morning by talking too much, so she hurried to the oven to save this batch. Even though a wave of heat enveloped her when she opened the oven, she still managed to listen to what Silvie had to say.

"My *mudder* sat me down when I first started being interested in boys. I could have been fifteen or sixteen. I'll never forget what she said to me." Silvie swallowed hard and her fragile complexion turned another shade of pale. "She said that there is no such thing as 'hearts and flowers' love between a man and a woman. I said, '*What about true love?*' And do you know what she said?"

Emma nibbled on the end of her fingernail, hoping that this batch hadn't been in for too long as well. "What did she say?"

"She said 'love shmuv' and then said, 'humpf.' What do you think of that?"

Emma shook her head. She was pleased that she and Silvie were growing closer as friends. "Some people do find true love; I found it twice."

"*Jah*, but John and I were never in love, because I never expected to find true love like you had with Levi, and now you have with Wil. John might have been in love with me, in his own way. My *mudder* insisted that things would go better for me if I weren't *deerich*, foolish, about love from the start and didn't expect too much." John, Silvie's husband, had died many years before.

"I guess some people don't find that special love, but a lot of people do. My *mamm* and *daed* are still very much in love; I'm sure of that," Emma said.

"I hope I find someone to love. It must feel good. Well, I mean I did love John in the end; I grew to love him as I would love any member of my *familye*."

"You're still young, Silvie. Why don't you ask *Gott* for a special *mann* to come into your life?" Emma studied Silvie's pretty face. She had the loveliest, pale creamy skin, which enhanced her pure blue eyes. She was truly an attractive woman.

"Do you think I should do that? It has always seemed selfish to me, to pray for something for myself instead of pray for someone else."

"I'm sure that *Gott* wants to hear about everything we care deeply about; He loves us so much."

Emma glanced at Silvie to see a smile float across her face.

"Are you two still talking?"

The girls looked up to see Wil standing in the doorway of the kitchen. Since Wil and Emma had started courting, Wil forgot about the need to knock and waltzed into the *haus* as he pleased.

Surely he could knock before he entered, Emma thought.

Wil took a seat at the kitchen table, reached out and took a sugar cookie. "Why did the conversation stop when I came in?"

The two girls smirked at each other.

Emma said, "We were talking about you."

Wil laughed and turned to Silvie. "Was Emma telling you how she can't wait to marry me?"

"Hush, Wil," Emma said quickly.

A look of delight crossed Silvie's delicate features. "Are you two getting married soon?"

"Eventually, but not right away." Emma was annoyed with Wil for saying such a thing to Silvie. Everyone they knew most likely suspected that they were courting, but it was only six months on from Levi's death, which was far too soon for a wedding. It was most likely far too soon to court and Emma struggled daily with the guilt of having feelings for another *mann* so soon. Emma often wondered why she loved Wil so much when she spent half her time being annoyed with him.

Wil laughed. "You know how I like to tease. Emma, do you have a cup of tea for me, or is this a ladies' only meeting?" Without drawing a breath, he added, "Are those chocolate chip cookies I smell?"

"*Jah* and I'll get you a cup of tea as soon as I put these cookies on a cooling rack."

While Emma tended to the cookies and got the tea, Wil bit into another sugar cookie and continued to speak to Silvie. "So, how have you been?"

"I've been fine. Busy at work that's all."

"I see."

Emma placed the tea in front of Wil, a little irritated that he had interrupted her girl-talk with Silvie.

Wil looked around to talk to Emma. "Since you won't marry me straight away, I've decided to take the bishop up on his offer."

"What offer?" Emma frowned. If they had private and important decisions to make, she would rather do that in private.

"There's a young man who wants to become Amish

and the bishop has asked if he can stay with me for a time. His name is Bailey Abler."

"That's odd," Emma said. "Don't they usually place people with a *familye* before they join?"

Wil shrugged his shoulders. "They normally do. He's been staying with the bishop for the past few days."

Given their conversation before Wil walked in, the girls shot each other a look of amazement. Was this new man *Gott's* answer so quickly, before Silvie had even had a chance to ask Him?

"How old is he?" Silvie asked, trying to keep the smile from her face.

"I haven't met him yet, but from what the bishop said, I'd guess him to be around thirty."

Emma put some of the warm chocolate chip cookies on a plate and placed it in the middle of the table before she sat down again. "What do you know about him?"

Wil wasted no time in taking one of the warm cookies. "Not much at all; the bishop hardly told me anything about him. He's alone in the world and used to work in the restaurant business. That's all I know."

"Well, I'm on the late shift at the bakery. I'd better get going." Silvie said.

"Late shift? I thought bakeries started around 3 a.m. in the mornings," Wil said before he took another bite of cookie.

"We've got a café attached now. We do light meals until 8 p.m. and I stay back and clean up afterwards too."

Wil wiped some crumbs from his mouth. "I see."

"You and Emma should come in and have dinner there one time," Silvie said.

Wil smiled at Emma. "Maybe we will."

After Silvie left, Wil said, "I've invited Frank to dinner on Saturday night."

Frank was an elderly man who lived on his own in one of the Amish housing settlements. Wil was one of the many Amish people who cared after him.

"So, does that include me?" Emma asked.

"Of course it does."

Emma giggled. "So, I do the cooking?"

Wil chuckled. "*Jah*. You cook much better than me."

Emma guessed that he wanted her to cook. She mostly cooked when he had guests for dinner, but he never asked her straight out, she always offered. "Who else is coming then?"

"That's all. Just you me, and Bailey will be here by then. I thought it would be *gut* for Bailey to get to know a couple of people to ease him into the community slowly."

"Why don't we have dinner here at my place instead of yours? I know my way around this kitchen so much better."

"*Jah*, okay. I'll call over and tell Frank that I've changed the dinner to your place. I can't do it today I've got too much to do. I'll do it tomorrow."

"I've got to go into town later. I'll call in and tell him if you like. I also think it wouldn't hurt to have Silvie over to meet Bailey. What do you think?"

"*Jah,* that will be fine, but don't you think you should meet Bailey first before you start planning to marry him off to someone?"

"I've just got a feeling about the two of them. Besides if he's made the decision to become Amish, he must have a *gut* heart toward *Gott*."

"And what is your feeling about you and me?" Wil moved next to Emma and pushed his shoulder against hers.

Emma giggled. "You know how I feel about you, Wil."

"Just checking, wouldn't want you to change your mind or anything." Wil stood up. "Well, I've got work to do.

Emma admired his strong, tanned arms as he reached for more cookies. "Another invention?"

Wil smiled. "I'll see you later on." He took two cookies off the plate, gave Emma a quick kiss on the forehead and walked out the door.

Emma wondered if she would have as much time with Wil when his *haus* guest arrived. She walked outside to bring the washing in off the line.

While she unpinned the washing, Emma's mind was drawn to the time when, as a young girl, she used to unpin the *familye* washing. She would pretend that her *bruders'* shirts were her sons' shirts. Emma had expected to marry and have many *kinner*. Emma knew that death was a part of life, and her grieving was eased by knowing where Levi was. But what of her plans of *kinner?* For so long she had dreamed of having children with Levi and now she had to switch her thinking to having children with Wil one day. Why did she struggle so much with that?

Chapter 2

*He that believeth and is baptized shall be saved;
but he that believeth not shall be damned.*
Mark 16:16

Emma pulled up her buggy in front of Frank's old wooden *haus*. The front garden had become a little overgrown, and Emma made up her mind then and there to get some of the ladies over to give his garden a *gut* weeding. Surely Frank wouldn't mind the company of a few ladies. Frank had lived alone since his wife, Sally, died years earlier.

As she knocked on the door, she noticed that the door could do with a repaint and remembered Wil had mentioned he would soon do some minor repairs on Frank's *haus*. She knocked again and waited a while, but still there was no answer. She figured that he could be out somewhere since many people in the community called on him. Maybe he had taken a walk. "Frank," she called out, but there was no answer.

She stepped out onto the street, and seeing no sign of him up or down the narrow road, she walked back up to the front door and turned the door handle. Frank was old and lived on his own; what if he had taken a fall?

The door was unlocked and Emma stepped through. "Frank," she called out once more. "You home?"

Emma immediately sensed that something was wrong. A step later she saw that the floor was covered with paperwork; the stuffing was pulled out of the couches, and drawers were pulled from cabinets. Emma knew that this was more than someone being untidy; it appeared as though Frank had been robbed. She called out his name again as she raced into one of the two bedrooms.

The mattress was shredded completely as if someone had ripped it with a knife; she ran to the other bedroom to see the same thing. She heard a clanging noise behind her and turned around. As she couldn't see anything, she slowly approached the kitchen. She ignored her fast pumping heart and before she looked around the corner into the kitchen, she glanced over her shoulder for an escape route. Seeing the front door open, she took a deep breath. *One, two, three, now*, she told herself as she stuck her head into the kitchen.

Emma heaved a sigh of relief; the noise she heard was just a cat. The large, gray tabby was busy lapping something from a saucepan on the stove. Emma moved toward the cat and it did not acknowledge her presence. "Shoosh, cat," Emma yelled. She flailed her arms to get it off the stove.

The cat remained as he was. Emma heaved up the cat into her arms and as she did so, she saw Frank spread out on the floor behind the kitchen table. Emma jumped and screamed, which caused the cat to yowl and jump from her arms. "Frank!"

Emma crouched over him. He was facing to the floor with one of his arms underneath him. Emma turned him over and felt for a pulse. It appeared that there was none. She guessed he had not been dead for long. Emma knew she would have to drive her buggy to the telephone shanty at the end of the road. Being in the midst of an Amish settlement, no one would have had a phone in their home.

After she made the phone call, Emma hung up the telephone. She looked down at her hands and could not stop them from shaking. She wanted nothing more but to tell Wil about Frank. Wil had a telephone in his barn, but was hardly ever in his barn and only used the telephone for outgoing calls. She called him anyway on the chance that he might be close to it, but as she suspected, there was no answer. She went back to Frank's *haus* to wait for the ambulance and the police, daunted that she would have to handle this all by herself.

When Emma got back to the *haus,* she peeped around the kitchen corner, a little scared to go back in. She saw that the cat was sitting on the kitchen table. She called to the cat, "Rude cat. Get off."

The cat looked at her, yowled and stayed put.

Emma tried a different approach. "Poor thing. Are you hungry?" Trying not to look at poor old Frank on the floor, Emma enticed the cat off the table with some cold meat she found in the cold box.

An ambulance and two police cars arrived within seconds of each other. Emma took the paramedics through to the kitchen; the uniformed police officers followed closely behind.

"Are you his next of kin?" one of the officers asked as the paramedics examined Frank.

"No, I'm just a friend. I know he has two sons, but I don't know how to contact them. A friend of mine would have their phone numbers; I'm sure of it."

Emma heard the paramedics murmuring between themselves about taking the body to the hospital.

"I guess you need to take him to a funeral home?" Emma asked.

"We'll take him to the hospital first, but we have to wait for the police."

"Ah, Mrs. Kurtzler, we meet again."

Emma looked around with a fright. "Oh, Detective Crowley. I didn't think I would see you again, so soon."

Crowley took out a notepad from his pocket. "Were

you the one to find the body?"

Emma did not like to hear Detective Crowley refer to Frank as *'the body.'* "Yes, I came and found Frank on the floor. He wasn't moving and I turned him over to feel for a pulse and couldn't find one." Emma heard people coming through the front door and looked up to see three people in white suits.

"Forensics," is all Crowley said then guided her into the living room.

Detective Crowley continued to stare at Emma, so she said, "I took the buggy up the road to find a public phone to call the police and the ambulance." Emma watched him scratch some things onto his notepad. She looked around for somewhere to sit, but the two couches were shredded.

"What brings you here, Detective? Do you come to every death in the area?"

"Death or murder?" He looked down into her eyes and then down to his notepad. "Why were you visiting him?"

"My… well, my friend and I were going to have Frank to dinner on Saturday night, but instead of having it at Wil's *haus* we were going to change it to have it at my *haus*. I was just coming here to tell Frank of the changed arrangements."

Detective Crowley scratched in his notebook. "Ah,

yes, William Jacobson."

She raised her eyebrows at the detective's memory. It would have been a *gut* six months ago when they met the detective. Emma recalled that Wil and the detective did not get along well.

"Did Frank have transportation?"

"*Nee*, he walks or someone in the community drives him where he needs to go."

"So Mr. Jacobson or yourself would have picked him up to take him to your house for dinner then drive him home again?"

Emma nodded. "That's correct."

After Crowley had penned some more things in his notepad, he looked up. "Why did he need to know of the changed arrangements? Couldn't you have picked him up and driven him to your place? If he wasn't driving himself, surely there was no need for the special trip to tell him of the change of the dinner location, was there?"

Emma chewed on a fingernail as she thought through what the detective had just said. He was right; there was no need to tell Frank at all since Wil would have driven him there and back. If only Wil didn't have his head in the clouds all the time. But, then again, she was also to blame. "I see. I guess I didn't think about it too much. Anyway he's an old man on his own; it doesn't hurt for people to call in on him every now and again."

"Hmm."

Emma wondered what *'hmm'* meant.

"Do you, or did you – I should say, know the deceased very well?"

"*Nee*, not that well. Wil knows him well and did a lot of things for him; like repairs and anything he needed done around the *haus*. He used to take him places, but so did others in the community. We look after our own, you know."

"Hmm, I know."

Emma studied the detective's sharp, angular facial features and figured that they matched the sharpness of his tongue and his blunt personality.

The detective walked around the living room and Emma followed him. As he circled one of the couches, he said, "It looks as though someone was looking for something, wouldn't you think? Someone's done a thorough search for something."

"Can I go now, detective? I'll have Wil call one of Frank's sons and I'm sure they'll take care of things."

As she walked toward the door, the detective said, "Mrs. Kurtzler, have you forgotten something?"

Emma spun around to face the detective. "No, I don't think I have."

Detective Crowley looked down at the cat that was

purring around his legs.

"Oh dear, the cat."

"Looks like it was the old man's cat. Why don't you take it home, Mrs. Kurtzler?"

"I can't have a cat. I've got enough animals to look after." She stared at the large tabby; he had stopped purring around the detective's legs and was staring at her, as was the detective. "I've never liked cats. Besides he'll likely chase all the birds that come into my garden."

"Don't trouble yourself. I'll call animal welfare and have it put down."

"No, you can't do that." The cat looked at her as if it knew exactly what the detective had said. Emma felt guilty and sighed. "All right. I'll take the cat." Emma crouched down. "Come on, kitty." The cat slowly walked toward her and did not object when Emma picked him up and tucked him under her arm. "Oh, he's such a heavy cat."

"Yes. It doesn't look like he's gone without too many meals."

"Well, goodbye, Detective."

"As usual, Mrs. Kurtzler, I will need to ask you some questions; don't leave town."

Emma headed to her buggy, glad to get away from the detective. She put the cat in the seat next to her, half hoping that he would jump out and run away. She'd had dogs before, but never a cat. Despite her hopes, the gray cat curled into a ball and immediately fell asleep. He looked so peaceful and cuddly that Emma felt bad for hoping he'd run away.

When she pulled up in front of Wil's *haus,* he came out to meet her.

"Wil, it's Frank."

"What's happened, Emma? You look as white as a sheet." Wil put his hands on Emma's shoulders to steady her.

"Frank has died. The police think that he's been killed. I found him on the kitchen floor and then waited for the ambulance to come. He had no pulse."

Wil's face was blank. "Is he dead?"

"Murdered, killed, *jah*, dead." Emma collapsed into his arms.

Wil held Emma tightly for a moment, before he said, "I should have gone. I never should have sent you."

"I offered to go. There shouldn't have been any harm in going. You weren't to know." Emma gave a couple of sniffs. "That horrible detective was there too."

"Crowley?"

Emma pulled her head back from Wil's shoulder. "That's the one. He said that from the look of the place that someone was searching for something."

Wil shook his entire body. "I'm having trouble taking it all in. Come and sit inside and tell me everything from the start."

Wil led Emma into his *haus*. She sat down and told him exactly what had happened, from start to finish.

"I'll have to find the phone numbers of his sons," Wil said.

"I thought you'd have their numbers."

"I think I do. *Jah*, I'm sure that I do."

Emma's hand flew to her forehead. "Oh, I forgot I've got Frank's cat."

"*Ach, gut*; Frank loved Growler. Where is he?"

"Asleep in the buggy. He was asleep when I left the buggy anyway." Emma looked out the window at the buggy and could not see a cat walking around anywhere.

"He's not a barn cat, Emma. You'll have to keep the cat in the *haus*. His name is Growler."

Emma pulled a face. "Growler? I suppose I can keep him in the *haus* just until one of Frank's sons come and get him."

"*Jah*, I'm sure one of them would love to take him."

Emma knew nothing of Frank's two sons, except that neither of them had stayed in the community. Both boys decided on the *Englisch* lifestyle many years ago. With Frank in his early eighties the boys would be in their fifties, Emma guessed.

As she usually did when she got home, Emma unhitched the buggy and tended to the horse. All the while Growler stayed in the buggy until Emma picked him up and carried him into the *haus*. Once inside, Growler jumped out of her arms, walked around the living room then sprung onto the couch, curled up and went back to sleep.

"You know how to look after yourself," Emma murmured to Growler. Emma put a couple of old saucers at the back door for his food and filled up a bowl with water.

Later that night Wil called in to Emma's *haus* to check on her. "You feeling better now?"

"*Jah, denke*. Have you had dinner?" Emma knew that Wil wasn't much of a cook and did not look after himself as he should.

"Have you?" Wil asked.

"I've just finished and I was in the middle of washing the dishes. Come into the kitchen." Emma continued to wash the dishes while Wil sat at the kitchen table. "Have you called Frank's sons yet?"

"*Jah*, Clive is out of the country and Andrew is coming tomorrow."

"*Gut*. What do you know about them?" Emma asked.

"Nothing. I remember them from years ago, but only

vaguely. Frank just gave me their phone numbers in case anything should happen to him."

"Was Frank expecting something to happen to him?"

"*Nee*, but he was old, that's all he meant. Even though his sons left, he still spoke to them. Well, from what he said, they hadn't visited him in five years, but he did get the occasional letter from them."

Emma nodded at what Wil said; she knew that many Amish parents had no contact with their *kinner* when they chose to leave the community, but it sounded as though it was the boys who did not keep in contact with Frank.

Wil said, "Why don't you come to Frank's *haus* tomorrow to meet Andrew?"

"I could, I guess. I'll ask if he can take Growler."

"Where is Growler?"

Emma looked around. "He was asleep on the couch last time I saw him." Emma looked by the back door to see that all the food had disappeared from the saucer. "Well, he's eaten." She pointed to the saucer. "That was full of food. I did leave the door open for a little while before, just in case he wanted to go out for a while. He might still be out there."

Wil jumped to his feet. "Emma, he might have run away."

"I have no litter tray. I had to let him out."

Wil went outside through the back door. "Here, Growler. Here kitty, kitty."

Emma followed him. "It's a little dark to see."

"Frank loved that cat," Wil said.

"Don't worry, we'll find him." Emma bit her lip and wished she'd taken better care of him.

After ten minutes of looking for him, they gave up. It was too dark to see too far.

"Hopefully, he'll be back in the morning," Emma said.

"*Jah*, I hope so. Night, Emma. Sweet dreams," Wil stepped in close to her.

"Night, Wil."

"It will be lovely when we can be together so I can cuddle you all night," Wil said as he put his arms around Emma's waist and pulled her to him.

Emma loved to feel his arms around her; she breathed in his masculine scent then giggled and pulled away. "Go on with you," she said with a laugh in her voice.

Wil walked down the road to his *haus*.

After Wil left, Emma felt a little better. It wasn't every day that she discovered a dead body and she was still a little shaken. There was also the unknown element of whether Frank died of natural causes or whether he was killed. She would hate to think that someone might have deliberately killed poor, old Frank.

Emma made sure that she locked and bolted the back door and the front door after what happened to old Frank. Emma re-boiled the kettle and made herself a chamomile tea hoping that it would help her sleep. She took the lamp up the stairs in one hand and her hot tea in the other ready for an early night. When she walked through her bedroom door, she saw Growler asleep in the middle of her bed. She hadn't even thought to look inside the *haus* for him. Emma laughed. "Make yourself comfortable, Growler."

Emma pushed Growler over to one side and thought it funny that he totally ignored her. Emma slipped under the covers, propped herself up with pillows and sipped her hot tea. She did want to share her bed once more with someone, but had hoped it would be with a *mann,* not a cat.

As she closed her eyes, Emma hoped that the widows would help her find out how Frank died.

Chapter 3

*Now faith is the substance of things hoped for,
the evidence of things not seen.*
Hebrews 11:1

As they walked from the buggy to the *haus,* Emma noticed that one of the neighbors was peeking through their window at them. Emma knew it was Thomas Graber.

Emma whispered to Wil, "Do you see Thomas Graber staring at us through the window?"

"Wouldn't be surprised. Frank and he never saw eye to eye on anything and recently they had quite an argument over a large fence that Thomas wanted to put up. Frank said that it would block the sunlight on his vegetables."

Emma looked at the messy front garden. "It's odd that the garden in the front is neglected and he spent all his time in the vegetable garden out the back."

"He loved his vegetables."

Wil and Emma waited in the *haus* and before too long a red sports car zoomed to a halt in front of the *haus.*

Andrew looked much like Frank except a younger version. He was tall and wide just like his *daed* had been. He had a younger woman with him and Emma wondered if she was Andrew's *dochder*.

"Nice to see you again, Wil," Andrew's voice boomed. He turned to Emma. "And who do we have here? I don't remember you and I'm sure I'd remember such a pretty face."

Emma smiled and wondered if Andrew was a salesman of some kind; he certainly knew how to compliment and flatter people. "Hello, I'm Emma. We've never met; I wasn't in the community when you were."

"Did you convert?" Andrew asked.

"*Nee*, I've always been Amish, but not from around these parts." Emma smiled at the girl on Frank's arm as she spoke.

"Oh, forgive my manners. This is my girlfriend, Lacey."

Emma noticed that Lacey was quite a fancy woman. She had shiny red lips, long red nails and her dress was way above her knees. Emma glanced at Lacey's four-inch heels and wondered how anyone could possibly walk in shoes that high.

Emma nodded hello to Lacey.

"Pleased to meet you, Lacey," Wil said before he

turned back to Andrew. "I would have hoped we would meet again under different circumstances. Let's talk inside the *haus*."

Andrew stepped inside the *haus* and turned about in a circle. "What a mess; apart from the mess, nothing has changed. Wil, how much do you think the *haus* would be worth? I'm not sure what the value would be."

"I don't know. Would you sell it or rent it?"

"I think Clive and I would want to sell. I've only spoken to him briefly; he's still overseas, but he'll back home in a week. I told him there's no need to rush home."

Emma was taken aback that the first questions Clive had were about the value of the *haus* rather than about how his *daed* died, but then again, he could have already talked to the police.

Wil lowered his head and asked, "Do you want us to delay the funeral 'til he gets here?"

"Wil, can you handle all that stuff, the funeral? Clive and I aren't Amish anymore and most likely won't even go to the funeral. If the community is happy to look after things, that would be good."

Wil remained silent. Emma knew that Wil was struggling with judgment. Surely, they would want to be certain that Frank would be buried in the same

Amish cemetery where Sally was buried, the one that they shared with the Mennonites. And why would they not attend their own *daed's* funeral?

"We'll cover the expenses, out of dad's estate. I'll have to go to the bank to see about his money. I'm guessing he had a stash of money since he sold the farm and bought this place after mum died. He would've had quite a sum left over."

"I'd say so. Well, if Clive and you don't want to be involved in the funeral, would you mind if we hold the service at my *haus*? The body is always in the *haus* for viewing and my *haus* is much bigger than this one. There'll be a fair crowd."

"Do whatever you want. Clive and I will have someone get the house ready for sale at some stage–clean it up and that sort of thing. Did dad have anything else of value?"

Lacey took a small step forward. "Like any antiques or jewelry?"

Wil laughed. "Lacey, Amish have no need of jewelry and if something is antique, it would have been something passed down through Frank's *familye*." Wil motioned with his hand toward the furniture in the living room. "Look around and see if you think the furniture is antique."

Lacey walked around the room looking at the odd

pieces of furniture scattered here and there. Lacey spun around to Andrew and said, "I don't care for any of it."

"It's not our style, Wil. I suppose it can be sold with the house. I'd dare say Clive wouldn't be interested in any of it either. It's basically junk."

Emma could not stop her eyebrows from rising. Lacey was far too interested in something that was hardly her business since she was only Andrew's girlfriend and not his *fraa*. Emma knew that Wil too would have been taken aback by Andrew and Lacey's manner. Andrew seemed to have no thought or care for his own father's funeral. "I'm looking after your *daed's* cat, Growler. Would you like him? I hear your *daed* was very fond of him."

Andrew held up a chubby hand and shook his head vehemently. "I don't want animals."

Emma looked to Lacey hoping she would say that she'd take the cat.

"I'm allergic to cat hair," Lacey said.

Of course, she would be allergic to cat hair, but not allergic to makeup, perfume, hair dye, acrylic nails and money, Emma thought before she could stop herself.

"So, Wil, anything else of value apart from this old house here?" Andrew asked.

Wil took his hat off and ran his hand through his hair, "He sold all the farm equipment at the same auction he sold the farm in. He sold the horses and the buggies. So that's it."

Andrew shook his head as if he was disappointed. Emma knew that Wil had to bite his tongue. Andrew seemed more concerned about the value of everything rather than the fact that neither he nor his *bruder* had visited their *daed* in the five years before he died.

Andrew took a handkerchief out of his pocket and mopped the sweat off his forehead. "Are you aware of any safe-deposit boxes my father had then? I'm sure he mentioned to me when I was a child that he had something special for us boys in a safe-deposit box."

Wil scratched his chin. "He told me nothing of the kind. Anyway, Andrew, Emma and I are very sorry for your loss."

Andrew nodded. "Thank you."

"I suppose the police have spoken to you about it all?" Emma asked.

"Yes, they think that he was startled by an intruder then fell and hit his head."

Emma raised her eyebrows once more. "Is that what they think?"

"Well, the place was trashed. I guess if there was anything of value here, it's well and truly gone by now," Andrew said then looked at Lacey who pouted her shiny, red lips.

"Wil, do you mind if I leave you in charge of letting a realtor through to look at the place, seeing that you live so close by and all?"

"Of course, Andrew."

"I'll have a realtor contact you in a week or two, or how ever long everything takes. I've never inherited anything before; I'm sure there will be probate and the property will have to be changed into our names before we sell."

Wil said, "I'm not sure how it works either; sorry I can't help you with that one."

"I'll be in touch then, thank you, Wil, Emma." Andrew and Lacey walked back to their red sports car.

* * *

The next night Emma met the widows at their regular gathering. They were a close-knit group that consisted of the two elderly sisters, Elsa-May and Ettie. Elsa-May was a large-busted, solidly built lady with a big dominating personality to go with it, whereas her *schweschder* was small and fine boned and a little timid, but no less shrewd. Also at their regular meetings were Silvie and Maureen, younger widows, only a little older than Emma.

As usual at their secret meetings there was a lot of food. There were chocolate fudge bars, chocolate brownies, cheesecake and cup cakes. Emma looked forward to the regular widows' meetings that they held, but she did not like the hard wooden chairs in the living room. Ettie and Elsa-May did not have a couch or a sofa; the two old ladies did not seem to miss having a couch one little bit. Emma wondered whether they had been brought up to sit on hard chairs and that's why they thought nothing of it - they had never known anything else. Emma knew that the younger widows found it uncomfortable as much as she by the way they kept moving and shifting in their seats.

"They're not releasing the body," Elsa-May said before she bit into a chocolate chip cookie.

"Frank's body?" Emma felt silly for asking such a thing as soon as she said it; there was no other 'body' in the community of which they would be speaking.

"*Jah*. The bishop told me that he organized for the funeral director to pick up the body, but they aren't releasing it."

Emma knew that Elsa-May was very *gut* friends with the bishop and his *fraa,* and regularly went to visit them.

Ettie leaned forward. "Obviously, they suspect foul play."

"Who would kill harmless old Frank?" Silvie slid forward slightly.

"I'm sure they'll find that it's all a mistake in a

couple of days," Maureen said.

Emma bit down on her lip. "The detective said that someone was looking for something."

"I hope poor old Frank didn't suffer," Ettie said. "More tea anyone?" Ettie rose to her feet and picked up the large china teapot and peered at each lady in turn.

Emma thought it amusing that Ettie referred to Frank as old; she was sure that Frank was younger than Ettie. "*Jah*, I'll have a top up, *denke*, Ettie." Emma stretched her hands as far as she could towards Ettie. She knew she risked being burned by hot tea as Ettie's shaking hands poured the tea into her cup.

"Do you remember seeing anything odd when you were at Frank's *haus*, Emma?" Elsa-May asked.

"He had some old soup or something of the kind on the stove; there were things all over the floor and the mattresses were shredded. That's all I can think of."

"Definitely sounds as though they were looking for something all right," Ettie said.

"They would've gone over the place for fingerprints already," Emma said.

"They won't find any fingerprints," Elsa-May said in a very firm voice. "The person who did this was looking for something and most likely something small since they shredded the mattresses." Elsa-May drummed her fingertips on her chin. "I wonder what old Frank could have been hiding."

"What do we know about Frank then?" Silvie said.

"He wasn't always Amish you know. He came to the community when he was in his late twenties. He married Sally soon after." Ettie gave a little giggle. "Tongues wagged when they got married so soon. Some said he only joined the community to marry Sally."

Emma dropped her gaze while she wondered if tongues would wag about her and Wil if they got married too soon. She was sure that they would.

"Sally was a little older than Frank, but he didn't seem to mind," Ettie said.

"What line of work was he in before he came to the community?" Maureen asked.

"That's a *gut* question dear, but I don't know. If I did know, then I've forgotten." Ettie turned to her older *schweschder*. "Do you know, Elsa-May?"

"It's such a long time ago and I was busy with my *kinner* and raising a *familye* back then. I didn't really pay much notice; I never spent much time in Sally's company. We were never that close with them were we, Ettie?"

"*Nee.*"

"He bought a farm and farmed the land. No one ever talked about what he did before, because his old life was buried when he got baptized," Elsa-May said with the hint of a smile on her face.

"I think the key to all this is what he did before he joined the community. We must find out what he did before," Emma said. "Can you Google him on your laptop, Ettie?"

The widows' giggled at Emma. "I know, I know. I was shocked when I first learned that Ettie had a laptop and Elsa-May had a cell phone, but we need to find out who did this to Frank. What if they haven't found what they want and they kill someone else?"

"We weren't laughing at you," Elsa-May said.

"If there was any other way we could investigate, we would use it," Ettie said. Ettie pulled out her laptop from the drawer in the dresser. She opened the lid and pressed some buttons and waited a while. "I'm afraid it's gone flat. I haven't charged it lately. I'll go into town tomorrow and use the electricity at the library to charge it."

"I distinctly remember telling you to always keep the thing charged," Elsa-May said firmly while glaring straight at Ettie.

"I will. I will. No need for anger. It goes flat over time; it's hardly my fault," Ettie said.

"I wasn't angry, Ettie. I just don't know why you can't keep the thing charged. I thought you would've learned that lesson by now. You remember that other time you didn't have it charged?"

"What time was that?" Emma knew these old ladies had done more investigating before, and investigating Henry Pluver's murder six months ago was not their first.

"Nothing, don't you worry about a thing, Emma. Ettie will have it charged tomorrow and we can all meet back here at the same time tomorrow night and find out Frank's background – that is, if there's anything about him on the internet."

"He's been Amish for so long that there may be nothing about him on the internet," Ettie said.

"We'll find that out then won't we, Ettie. But now, we'll have to find that out tomorrow instead of tonight because you didn't have it charged."

Ettie hung her head then closed the lid of her laptop. "*Jah*, sorry Elsa-May."

"Well, do it tomorrow, Ettie." Elsa-May shook her head at her *schweschder's* incompetence.

"Can we meet the day after tomorrow?" Emma knew she was brave making such a request. She did not want Elsa-May's attitude toward her *schweschder* to transfer to her. She added quickly, "I've got Wil and someone who's staying with him coming to dinner tomorrow night and Silvie will be there too."

"Do tell," Maureen said.

Emma giggled, remembering she hadn't told Maureen about Bailey. "There's a man who wants to join the Amish and the bishop asked Wil if he could stay with him for a while before he makes the decision to get baptized. He's been staying with the bishop for the last few days." Emma turned to Elsa-May. "Did you meet him at the bishop's *haus*, Elsa-May?"

Elsa-May looked away from Emma as she spoke. "*Nee*, I haven't met him yet. I know of him, that's all. He was out in the fields when I visited recently. Well, everyone all right to meet the night after next?"

Everyone agreed to meet back at Elsa-May and Ettie's *haus*.

Chapter 4

Even so faith, if it hath not works, is dead, being alone.
James 2:17

Emma relaxed on her porch. She had just cleaned her *haus* from top to bottom and she planted some snow peas, pumpkin and squash. She figured she deserved a little break while dinner cooked. Today Wil was coming to dinner with the new man, Bailey. She had vegetables and chicken roasting in the oven.

She looked across her farm that was once leased by Henry Pluver and was now leased and farmed by his son, Bob. Bob kept to himself and that suited Emma just fine. He seemed to be doing a *gut* job since taking over his *daed's* leases and had even employed a couple more people to help him. Wil told her that he was going to try and get Bailey a job with Bob, or have him work for Bob for no pay, just to see what it was like to work on an Amish farm and mix with the Amish folk.

Maybe with Bailey living with him, Wil wouldn't come around as much. Emma smiled at how Wil would call in to see her at odd times; it never entered his head that some times may not be convenient. How different her late husband, Levi was to Wil. Levi was grounded and practical whereas Wil had his head in the clouds most of the time.

How funny it was that she could find love with two totally different *menner.* Levi was all about work, even when he was at home he found things to work on. Wil was happy to live on the income that came to him from leasing out his farm and from his investments. Wil lived life at a much slower pace than Levi had. Wil found enjoyment with his tinkering with silly inventions. Levi had always seen Wil's inventions as a complete waste of time and energy.

Emma looked to the trees on the horizon. She noticed how the sky just above the trees was much paler than the sky up higher. The sky high in the sky was the bluest of blue. She looked over the wheat that gently blew in the breeze. Peace filled her being as she closed her eyes and pushed all thoughts and worries out of her mind.

Silvie was the first to arrive and interrupted Emma's quiet time. After she tied up her horse, she walked toward Emma.

"Hello, Silvie. Come and sit with me for a while. Wil and Bailey haven't arrived yet and I don't have to do anything with the dinner for a few more minutes."

"I brought some apple pie and bread. I'll just take it into the kitchen."

When Silvie returned, she slumped into the porch chair beside Emma.

"You seem tired, Silvie."

"I've done a lot of work today. I worked this morning at the baker's and then I did some chores this afternoon. There's a lot to do when you live by yourself and don't have someone to help you and these odd shifts are a lot to handle. Sometimes I'm on the late shift and then the early shift. It doesn't give me much time to sleep."

"I guess I'm blessed to have Wil help me with things," Emma said.

"*Jah*, and Maureen has her *bruder,* John, do things for her."

"Silvie, if you have anything you need done, just say so. Wil would happily do anything and I'm sure John would too."

Silvie forced a laugh. "Well, it's mainly the little things. Like have someone make me a cup of tea when I'm feeling poorly. Or have someone feed the animals once in a while."

"*Gott* will have someone for you, don't be concerned, and just trust."

Silvie nodded. "I have been trusting, but I'm starting to worry that I'm getting too old to have *kinner*. What if *Gott* doesn't bring me someone until I'm too old? You know it gets harder to conceive the older you get."

Emma bit her lip and looked across her farm. "I've always wanted *kinner* too. I used to take it for granted that I would have some one day." She had pushed thoughts of *kinner* right out of her mind. Maybe she was doing the wrong thing in keeping Wil at arm's length for so long while she waited an acceptable time before marrying him, but what if in so doing she was destroying her chances of having *kinner?*

"I didn't mean to worry you, Emma."

Emma turned to look at Silvie. "You're right, Silvie. I've heard that too, about being too old to conceive. It seems that older women in the community don't have a problem conceiving if they've already had *kinner,* but first timers like we are have trouble if it's their first. Oh dear, you know what I mean, don't you?"

"*Jah*, I do. If a woman in her late thirties has already got four *kinner* she has another easily, whereas if it's her first it's harder."

Emma nodded. "Exactly. I don't know why that is, but I've noticed that pattern of things before."

"Me too," Silvie said.

"We can't worry about those things though. If *Gott* blesses us with *kinner,* we will have them, but if not then that's not in His plan for us. We can't worry about it."

Silvie smiled a tight-lipped smile.

Emma said, "Look at the beautiful view, the colors the gentle swaying of the trees in the breeze. Listen to the birds."

After a moment Silvie said, "I don't take enough time to appreciate the simple things."

"Me either, we should do more of it."

"When do you think you and Wil might marry? He'd marry you tomorrow. I'm sure of it."

Emma chewed the end of her fingernail. "It's too soon, don't you think? It's only been six months since Levi died."

"If you love him, I don't see that there's anything wrong with it," Silvie said.

"People might talk. I just want to do the right thing I don't want people to talk about me."

"What would the right time be? What if Wil doesn't wait for you?"

Emma laughed. "I know that he'll wait for me. We are committed to each other in that way; he knows I'll marry him at some point."

After a moment's silence, Silvie asked, "Do you need any help with the dinner?"

"*Jah*, come on let's go inside." Both women stood up and went inside.

Moments later there was a knock on the door. Emma was surprised. *Could this be Wil, knocking all of a sudden rather than barging in?*

Emma opened the door. "Wil."

"Hello, Emma. This is Bailey."

"Hello, Bailey; pleased to meet you. Please, come in. Come through to the kitchen, dinner is nearly ready."

Emma's kitchen was huge, plenty big enough for the long table, which could comfortably sit twelve people, but today she had one end of it set for the four of them.

Emma watched Silvie's face as she looked at Bailey. It was obvious from the look in Silvie's eyes that she found Bailey pleasing to look at. Emma turned to study Bailey and saw that he had the same look on his face. Wil introduced the two of them.

Bailey was a very good-looking man. He was tall with a medium build, thick light brown hair that was cut in a typical *Englisch* cut with short sideburns, parted at the side with a little length on top. He appeared to have a day's growth of whiskers. Emma could see why Silvie was so taken with him. To top everything off, he had a beautiful smile.

Everyone sat at the table and Emma placed the roasted chicken, vegetables and the cold cuts in the middle of the table, so each could help themselves. There were two fresh loaves of seeded bread that Silvie had brought from the bakery where she worked.

Wil said to Bailey, "You probably already know that

we each say our own silent prayer of thanks to *Gott* before we eat?"

Bailey nodded and closed his eyes.

Once everyone had finished giving thanks they opened their eyes and began to eat.

Bailey helped himself to chicken and some roasted sweet potato.

"What made you want to join the community, Bailey?" Emma asked.

"I've been doing a lot of thinking about life and God and I could see that I was living a shallow life with no meaning. I came to realize that what's important is God's salvation."

Silvie giggled. "You'll have to learn to speak Pennsylvania Dutch."

"I can do that. I don't think that will be a problem. You could help me."

Emma secretly smiled at the way the two of them were speaking to one another. It was clear that they were attracted to each other and very much so. Emma hoped that this was the right man for Silvie.

They would certainly have beautiful *bopplis*. Bailey's hair would have surely been blonde as a child and his eyes were as blue as Silvie's.

But, they would have to wait a while if they were interested in one another. Bailey had yet to be baptized and would have to wait a time to see if he wanted to live the Amish ways.

Ideally, Bailey should not be influenced by the love of a woman. But what was ever ideal? It wasn't ideal for Levi to die and leave her childless and alone. Did anyone ever lead an ideal life or live the life that they imagined for themselves? Surely disappointment and struggle was a part of life.

Wil quickly swallowed the food in his mouth. "Bailey, it's an important commitment. If you decide to join you will have to commit before the whole church to serve *Gott* with your heart, soul, mind and body. You will be bound to that for life."

"The bishop has explained it all to me, Wil. I've already made that decision it's just the bishop I'm waiting on. He says I have to wait a time. He didn't tell me how long I must wait before being baptized. I'd be baptized tomorrow if I could."

"*Nee*, it would be far too soon. You'd only have an idealized view of what being Amish is. You have to live it to know it." Wil put his fist to his heart.

Emma stared at Wil; she had never heard Wil speak so definite on any matter.

"I'll have to take your word on that since I haven't lived it much so far," Bailey said.

Chapter 5

Thou shalt not make unto thee any graven image, or any likeness of any thing that is in heaven above, or that is in the earth beneath, or that is in the water under the earth.
Exodus 20:4

When their visit with Emma was over, Wil and Bailey walked home.

"Wil, what should happen if I want to take a lady on a date?"

Wil laughed. "Silvie?"

"You noticed?"

Wil nodded.

"How do I get to know her better; how do the Amish do that?"

Wil scratched his chin. "I don't know if you should be distracted by a woman at this stage, Bailey. Did the bishop tell you that you should learn our ways first?"

"I know I shouldn't, but it's a bit hard not to be distracted by a beautiful woman. I'll keep my intentions honorable of course."

Wil slapped Bailey on the shoulder. "What we do is take them on a buggy ride or sometimes we take them out for a meal, as the *Englisch* do."

"A buggy ride sounds the thing to me, nice and romantic."

"Do you know how to drive a buggy?"

"*Jah.* The bishop showed me how to hitch a buggy and drive one. I know all the road rules too."

"*Wunderbaar.* You can take one of my buggies."

"Thank you, Wil. I'll do that. Should I call on her? Do you know where she lives?"

Wil hoped he was doing the right thing and would not get into trouble with the bishop. "*Jah*, it's the old red *haus* just before you turn onto the road that takes you into town. Don't get too interested in her though; you're supposed to learn our ways first." Although Wil considered he should have dissuaded Bailey, he knew what it was like to love a woman and he found it difficult to stand in love's way.

"I might call on her tomorrow."

"One more thing, Bailey. The Amish, I suppose you know, are not physical before marriage."

"I know that, Wil. I'll be a gentleman."

Wil was a little concerned; he hardly knew Bailey and if anything went wrong he would hold himself responsible.

Once they arrived back at Wil's *haus*, Bailey went up to his bedroom and Wil stayed downstairs in the living room. Wil hoped that Emma would accept his proposal of marriage soon. She had said that she would marry him, but had given him no timeframe. He would wait for her because he understood that it was important for her to be ready to love him fully, but that did nothing to stop his yearnings for her.

* * *

Silvie was sweeping her small patio when she heard a buggy. Her heart raced when she saw that the man driving the buggy was Bailey.

Her hands flew to straighten her apron and prayer *kapp* before she stepped down to meet him. "Bailey, this is a nice surprise."

Bailey got out of the buggy. "Hello. I hope you don't mind me calling in on you like this."

"Not at all."

"Would you come on a buggy ride with me sometime?"

Silvie was delighted and a little shocked. It had been years since she had been asked such a thing. She wanted to look away and laugh, but she could not keep her eyes from him. "I'd like that."

"How about now?"

"Right now?" Silvie's heart beat faster and harder. She would have preferred some time to lead up to this, but then if she had time to think she may refuse his offer.

"Why not? I'm sure your sweeping can wait. Come with me now." Bailey held out his hand.

Silvie looked at her *haus*, stifled a giggle and then said, "All right."

A huge smile spread across Bailey's face, which made him even more handsome.

Once they were both in the buggy, Bailey said, "Now, you'll have to tell me which way to go because I don't know these roads yet."

"Go left at the top of this road. I can show you around a little." Silvie took him on some quiet roads in the hope that too many people would not see them. Her late husband, John, had been gone for some time and Silvie knew that she was ready for the *mann* that *Gott* had chosen for her. Maybe it was Bailey. She looked across at him and he smiled back at her.

"Do you have *bruders* or *schweschders*, Bailey?" Silvie hoped that Bailey would be close with his *familye*.

"I know that means brothers and sisters and yes, I have two *bruders* and two *schweschders*, but I haven't spoken to them in years. What about you?"

"I have five older *bruders*, and one younger *schweschder*. I'm from Ohio originally. John, my late husband, and I moved here just after we got married.

There were more job opportunities here for him." Silvie's shoulders drooped slightly as she remembered John.

Bailey took his eyes off the road and glanced over at her. "I'm sorry; no one told me that you'd lost your husband."

Silvie gave a nervous laugh. "Amish get married very young; I know that's not the same for the *Englisch.* Most of us get married before twenty years of age. It would be a little unusual for someone of my age never to have been married. Of course, there's the odd one who never marries." Silvie wanted the conversation away from herself. "Have you ever considered marriage, Bailey?"

"I'm divorced." He glanced at her just in time to see her purse her lips. "What was that look for?"

Silvie felt heat rise to her cheeks. "I didn't mean to have such a reaction. It's just that there's no divorce amongst the Amish."

"I know. The bishop told me all about things like that. The bishop said that I wouldn't have been allowed to enter an Old Order Amish community because of the divorce. He said if a couple really cannot get along, rather than divorce they live separately, but divorce is not an option. Since I was an *Englischer* when I divorced, the bishop is prepared to overlook my first marriage. He said that the past sin is washed away by baptism and repentance."

"That's right; marriage is forever. So it's important to make the right choice to start with."

"Would you ever get married again, Silvie?"

Silvie took a slow deep breath. "John died years ago and for the first few years I knew I would never marry again, but lately I've been thinking that it would be nice to have someone to look after and someone to cook for." Silvie noticed that Bailey smiled.

"That's good," he said.

"You drive the buggy very well for an *Englischer*."

"The bishop gave me a few lessons and Wil made sure I could drive before he let me loose with one of his horses." Bailey ran his eyes over the countryside. "It's so peaceful out here. Why don't we go for a walk?"

"Okay, it's a perfect day for it."

Bailey tied the horse up to the side of a fence post. "It's so quiet and peaceful out here and the air is so fresh."

Silvie glanced up into his face as they walked. She could see herself falling in love with this man, but she had to wait. She would not give her heart too quickly. She would wait until he was baptized and integrated into the community.

"Did you know, old Frank, the man who died?" Bailey asked.

Silvie held her long dress up just a little so it would not trail along the long grass. "Just a little. It was horrible what happened to him, but he's gone home to be with the Lord so he'll be happy now."

Bailey stopped walking. "You know that for sure, do you?"

Silvie stopped as when Bailey had. Warning bells went off in her head; it sounded like this man was having problems believing. "Of course I know that for sure. I know it in my heart."

Bailey put a finger to his chin. "What if it's all not real?"

"Bailey, if you have doubts like that, then what are you doing here?"

He looked up to the sky and back to look into her face. "I believe in my heart, but I have – sometimes I have a tiny doubt. That's allowable, isn't it?"

"*Nee*, I don't think so. It's a real commitment for an *Englischer* to become Amish. Being Amish is so much more than wearing these clothes, living simply and driving a buggy. We live our lives for *Gott* with all our heart, mind and soul. Where there is doubt then faith is not there. You have to believe with faith and block out any doubt." Silvie licked her lips and hoped that she was getting through to him. "It's only fear that causes the doubt."

"I'm just being honest with you, Silvie. I guess you're right. The Scripture says perfect love casts out fear. Perfect love of *Gott* causes fear to run away."

Silvie smiled at him quoting Scriptures. "That's right. Just believe that's all we have to do. It's not hard."

"*Denke*, Silvie."

Hearing that Bailey was divorced, Silvie knew she would have to wait a while if this was the *mann Gott* had for her. She did not want to become the second woman that Bailey divorced. *Maybe Gott is testing me with this mann, testing my faith,* Silvie thought.

Bailey looked up again, to the sky. "I don't think I've ever heard so many birds chirping. And so many different birds."

Silvie closed her eyes and listened to them. "*Jah*, I didn't even hear them until you mentioned them."

Bailey pulled on her arm. "Let's sit over here and listen to them."

The two of them sat on a large boulder and closed their eyes. The sun warmed their faces and a gentle and cool breeze enveloped them as they listened to the birds make music.

As she opened her eyes, Bailey took hold of her hand. She pulled her hand away. "It's too soon, Bailey."

"What's too soon, Silvie?"

"It's too soon for anything like this. You and me."

Bailey moved closer to her. "How long will I have to wait?"

Silvie's body stiffened. "It's not about waiting."

"Then why should I wait? I know what my heart wants."

Silvie covered her mouth and giggled. "We've only just met."

Bailey gave her a smile that melted her heart. If *Gott* was testing her, he picked an excellent *mann* with whom to test her. "There's a bigger decision you have to make first and that decision should not be clouded by me."

He chuckled. "Too late for that."

Silvie put her head down and looked into her hands. "Maybe we should go back."

"Maybe we should stay here."

She looked up and stared into his eyes for some time before she could take his gaze no longer. Silvie looked straight ahead into the fields. She could see out of the corner of her eye that Bailey was still staring at her.

"You are the most beautiful woman I've ever seen, Silvie. Not only that, you're kind and sweet as well."

His words could have sounded insincere, but the way he said them made Silvie sure that he meant every one of them. Silvie rose to her feet. If she stayed sitting any longer she just might have to kiss him and she knew that would be the wrong thing to do. "We should be getting back."

"*Nee*, sit with me a little longer, please? Let's enjoy this beautiful day that *Gott* has given us."

Silvie sat down again. "Just for a little longer then."

"Have you known Wil and Emma long?"

Silvie was pleased of a change of subject. "*Jah*, I've known them since I moved here, but I was never close with them until Emma's husband died. Now that we're both widows we have something in common."

Bailey nodded. "And you didn't know Frank well?"

"*Nee*, not well at all." Silvie was sure that it was the second time that Bailey had asked her about Frank. "Why do you ask?"

"Just interested in everyone, that's all."

Silvie wanted to know why Bailey got divorced. Did his wife want the divorce or did he? She did not ask because she did not want to speak of unpleasantness. "What kind of work will you do here in the community?"

"I've always worked in restaurants. I've owned a few, but Wil has the idea that I should work on a farm to get to know other Amish men and see what the traditional Amish man does."

Silvie could not see the sense in what Wil had advised him to do. "But you're not the traditional Amish man."

"I know, but I have to do something, start somewhere.

I have to prove myself; I have to prove that I'm a hard worker."

Silvie nodded. "What do your *familye* think of you living here?"

"I don't have much contact with them."

Bailey's face hardened as he spoke of his *familye*.

"That's sad," she said.

"Why didn't you move back to Ohio after your husband passed away?"

"This is my home now. I need to go forward with my life not backwards. I miss my *familye*, but I have the community here and they're like my *familye*. The community will become your new *familye* too. If you stay, you'll see what I mean."

"Of course I'll stay. I would have been baptized straight away only the bishop wouldn't let me."

Silvie looked into his eyes. She hoped that he would take hold of her hand again, but he didn't. "I suppose the bishop knows that there will be some big changes for you and you might not like them."

"*Jah*, I know. I know his reasoning."

Silvie could tell by the way he looked into her eyes that he was smitten with her. She glanced at his lips and wondered what they would feel like on hers. "We should go."

"All right, we'll go." Bailey stood up and held out

his hand.

Silvie put her hand in his and rose to her feet.

"We will go back as soon as we go for another walk. It's a shame to ignore this beautiful countryside."

Seeing that Bailey still had hold of her hand and was walking away, Silvie had no choice but to go with him.

They walked for fifteen minutes and on their return to the buggy Bailey stopped still and picked up Silvie's hand. "Silvie, I need to tell you that I want to kiss you. I know I can't and I'm showing great restraint."

Silvie looked into his face. He spoke with such sincerity that she knew that he was a *gut* man and one who could be trusted. A nervous sound escaped from the back of Silvie's throat. She wanted to be held tightly in his strong arms. She forced herself to say, "We have to wait."

He drew her hand to his lips and looked into her eyes as he pressed his warm lips into the back of her hand. The touch of his lips sent tingles spiraling through her body. She giggled nervously and pulled her hand away. "We must get back."

He stood still watching her while she climbed into the buggy. "*Kumm*, Bailey."

Bailey let out a noisy sigh, untied the horse and climbed into the buggy.

All the way back to her place Silvie regretted not

kissing him. *What harm could a tiny kiss do?* It had been so long since she'd been kissed. She had kept away from *menner* since John died. Bailey was the first *mann* to hold her interest.

"Well, here you are." Bailey pulled up the horse in front of Silvie's door.

"*Denke* for a nice time, Bailey."

With one strong arm, Bailey took hold of her behind her waist and pulled her quickly to him. Silvie did not resist and before she knew what was happening, his lips were softly against hers. He released her at once. "Forgive my boldness."

Silvie made an attempt at a smile and shook her head. She quickly got out of the buggy and swallowed hard. "Bye, Bailey."

He nodded his head and clicked the horse forward.

Silvie put her hand to her fast beating heart and hurried into the safety of her *haus*.

Chapter 6

*But the fruit of the Spirit is love, joy, peace,
longsuffering, gentleness, goodness, faith,
Meekness, temperance:
against such there is no law.
And they that are Christ's have crucified the flesh with
the affections and lusts.*
Galatians 5:22-24

As arranged, the widows met once again and this time they were to hear what Ettie had found out from the internet, about Frank.

Emma was the first to speak. "What did you find out, Ettie? Anything?"

"It's convenient that one of Frank's relatives has researched the family history. Frank's father was an art dealer back in the old country and before Frank came to join us he worked at an auction house in Chicago as an auctioneer."

"What sort of auction house?" Emma asked.

"Seems to be an art auction house as far as I can tell. I looked them up and they don't sell anything but paintings."

"So, he followed in his father's footsteps." Maureen

tried to lean back in the chair.

"It appears so," Ettie said.

"Anything else, Ettie?" Silvie asked.

"*Nee*. I've asked the people in the community who knew him best and he never spoke of his life before he joined us," Ettie said.

"Maybe someone thought that he had a valuable painting hidden or something. Maybe it was a stolen painting," Maureen said.

"Excellent point, Maureen, but I already thought of that. There are too many to track though. There are many, many missing paintings from Germany during the war and there are many stolen paintings over the years from Chicago. So even if he did have a stolen painting, we would have no way of knowing which one he had."

"It sounds all very far fetched," Silvie said. "It could have just been random thieves after money. Remember that it's often the most logical explanation that is the right one," Silvie said.

"Random thieves don't kill people though, Silvie. Thieves run if they're seen. They don't usually turn around and kill people," Elsa-May said.

"Wil's going to have Frank's body at his *haus* for the viewing and everything. Frank's sons don't want to be involved in the funeral," Emma said.

"Why don't we clean Frank's *haus* and that way we can look for clues?" Ettie said.

"Great idea, Ettie," Elsa-May said.

"The police have combed right through it, doubt there will be any clues left," Emma said.

"*Jah*, but we have to start somewhere," Elsa-May said.

As they were getting into their buggies, Silvie shared with Emma that she went on a buggy ride with Bailey.

"Silvie, I know he's handsome, but he's not even properly one of us yet. Don't you think you should wait?" Emma asked.

"I should, I know, but it's hard."

Emma nodded and said goodbye to Silvie. On her way home anger welled up within her. Wil had to know of it because he would have use of one of Wil's buggies. Emma called in on Wil on her way home.

Wil answered the knock on his door. "Emma, come in."

"I would prefer to speak out here." She spoke in a low tone so Bailey would not hear her. "I just heard from Silvie about her time with Bailey."

Wil nodded.

"Don't you think it's a bit soon for him to be taking someone for a buggy ride? What would the bishop think of that?"

Wil remained silent, so Emma continued, "Bailey's been entrusted into your care. Can't you take anything seriously, Wil?"

Wil rubbed his forehead. "I know what it's like when you love someone, Emma."

Emma scoffed. "Love? They've only just met."

"What about us?" Wil asked.

"I'm not speaking of us."

"You never want to speak of us, Emma."

"It's things like this that make me unsure about you, Wil, if I have to be truthful."

Wil raised his eyebrows and stepped closer to her. "What do you mean?"

"I need someone in my life who'll be stable and solid and not do things without thinking. You surely did not think things through if you gave Bailey a buggy to take Silvie out. What about Silvie, what if she gets hurt?"

"Sometimes people have to take a chance, Emma. That includes you. Now, if you'll excuse me. I've some things to do before I turn in for the night."

"What? Like a silly invention?" Emma bit her lip as soon as she said it. She went to say sorry, but Wil spoke before she had a chance.

"Goodnight, Emma." Wil closed his door.

Chapter 7

Therefore I say unto you, Take no thought for your life, what ye shall eat, or what ye shall drink; nor yet for your body, what ye shall put on. Is not the life more than meat, and the body than raiment? Behold the fowls of the air: for they sow not, neither do they reap, nor gather into barns; yet your heavenly Father feedeth them. Are ye not much better than they?
Which of you by taking thought can add one cubit unto his stature?
Matthew 6:25-27

Emma arrived early at Wil's home the day of the funeral, as did Maureen. They were fixing the food for the people who would want to return there from the cemetery for a light meal. Maureen and Emma decided on cold-cuts coleslaw and two hot dishes. Meals after a funeral were never a lavish affair.

The bishop and the ministers were the first to arrive. It wasn't long before there were rows of buggies outside Wil's *haus*.

"Look at everyone, Maureen. I'm glad Wil decided to have the service held here because Frank's *haus* would have been far too small for all these people."

Maureen looked out the kitchen window. "Well, we've done all we can do in here for the time being. Let's go and greet some people."

The two ladies left the kitchen and went into the living room where everyone had gathered. The minister, rather than the bishop gave a short talk on life and death. Explaining that it was all a cycle, birth death and it was a natural thing that everyone has to go through.

Maureen and Emma sat next to each other and Emma saw that Maureen's eyes misted over and Emma knew that she was thinking of her late husband. She squeezed Maureen's hand. Emma coped with her own grief by trying not to think too much of Levi. It was hard but she kept as busy as she could rather than face the pain of her loss. Emma could only keep reminding herself that Levi was in a better place.

After the viewing everyone got into their buggies to follow the funeral buggy to the cemetery.

After prayers were said, the coffin was lowered into the ground. Emma looked up and noticed Elsa-May and Ettie standing next to Silvie. Wil and Bailey were standing in a group with some of the men.

Emma and Maureen knew that they would have to be the first to leave so they could go back to Wil's *haus* to get the meal ready. As they both turned around they saw that Bob Pluver had been standing directly behind them. Emma immediately got the chills. Bob Pluver was such an odd character.

"Hello, Maureen and Emma," Although he addressed Emma as well, his eyes were focused the whole time on Maureen.

"*Ach*, hello, Bob." Maureen glanced across at Emma. "Um, did you know Frank very well?"

"*Jah* I did."

Emma had to fight the smile that was trying to spread across her face. It was clear that he had a liking for Maureen because this was the most she'd ever heard Bob say unless he was talking farm business.

"Were you friends with him, Bob?" Maureen asked.

Bob nodded.

"*Gut* friends?"

"I'd say so." Bob folded his arms in front of him and leaned back.

"Did you visit him much?" Emma asked.

"I visited him every Thursday."

Emma realized that Bob must have been at Frank's *haus* on the very day that he died, but this was hardly the time or the place to ask him questions. She would have Maureen ask him questions tomorrow.

"He was a nice man," Bob said slowly.

"*Jah*, he was a nice man. I didn't know him well, but I'm sure he was a nice man," Maureen gave him a big hearty smile revealing the slight gap in between her front teeth. "If you can excuse us, Bob, we have to go and prepare the meal back at Wil's *haus*. You're very welcome to come join us, Bob."

Bob smiled at Maureen. "*Jah* I'll come, *denke*."

As they hurried to the buggy, Emma said, "That's the most I've ever heard him say. I think he's sweet on you. He couldn't take his eyes from you and also that's the first time I've ever seen him smile. He looks a different person when he smiles."

Maureen smiled and hunched her shoulders. "He's a sweet boy."

Emma thought she could think of a few other descriptions for him other than sweet, but she kept her opinions to herself. "He'd have to be our age, wouldn't he, Maureen?"

Emma was in her late twenties and Maureen was in her early thirties, Emma was sure of that.

As they travelled back to Wil's *haus*, Emma said, "Be careful then if you don't want an admirer, Maureen."

* * *

Silvie was still at the funeral. Bailey had been on her mind every second of every day she looked for him and saw him talking to some people. She walked over so she would be close to him, hoping that he would speak to her. As soon as Bailey saw her he excused himself from the couple he was speaking with.

"Hello, Silvie."

His smile melted her heart. "Hello. What did you think of your first Amish funeral?" Silvie asked.

"Pretty much the same as the other funerals I've been too. Not too different."

There was an awkward silence as Silvie searched for something to say.

Bailey leaned into her and spoke softly, "I enjoyed our buggy ride."

Silvie nodded and felt her cheeks heat up. She knew she was blushing and she hoped that Bailey did not notice. "Me too."

"Do you know everyone here?" Bailey asked.

Silvie looked around. "*Jah*, I think I do. Or at least I've seen all these people before. I may not be able to tell you all their names. I would've expected Frank's sons to be here and they don't appear to be."

"*Nee*. Wil told me that the sons said they wouldn't be coming to the funeral. They asked Wil to look after things."

Silvie raised her eyebrows in surprise at his sons being so disinterested in their father that they could not even go to his funeral.

Bailey spoke softly. "It seems a little odd, doesn't it? That they don't even want to go to their father's funeral, to pay their respects?"

"It is very odd. Maybe they feel awkward because they left the Amish; they might feel they have no place here."

"Maybe. Wil said they hadn't visited Frank for some years," Bailey said.

"*Jah*, that's what I heard." After a small silence, Silvie said, "I'll see you at Wil's *haus* then." Silvie turned and walked away. She could feel Bailey's eyes on her as she walked. She dare not turn around.

* * *

There were some hundred folk gathered at Wil's *haus*. Emma kept herself busy in the kitchen in an effort to avoid Wil. When the people had nearly all gone home, Maureen, Silvie and Emma stayed back to clean up afterwards.

Emma looked out the kitchen window and saw that Wil was outside saying goodbye to some people. She took her opportunity. "We've nearly finished. Do you two mind if I leave you to finish off?"

Both girls looked at her as though they wondered what she was up to. Any other time she would have wanted to stay back to have more time with Wil. She did not want to share with them that she'd had a little tiff with him. "I've got some things I need to take care of at home," she explained.

"Of course, go," Maureen said.

Emma wrapped a portion of left over meat for Growler and slipped out the back door and hurried home.

As she opened her front door, Growler was sitting there as if he was waiting for her. "Hello, I brought you some meat."

Growler meowed and walked toward her.

"Over to your saucer, then." The cat followed Emma to the saucer at the back door. Growler appreciated the meat. Emma smiled as she watched him eat it. Even though she did not like cats she was beginning to see why some people did. It was nice to come home and have someone waiting for you even if it was a cat who ignored her most of the time.

Emma filled up the kettle and placed it on the stove. A nice cup of meadow tea would be just what she needed. As she rinsed out the cup in the sink, she remembered that day at Frank's *haus* when she found him; there were two cups in the sink. Why would he need two cups? He must have had a visitor there that day and it must have been someone that he knew. If someone had come to steal from him, he would not sit down and have a cup of tea with him.

Finished with his meat, Growler jumped on the chair next to her and looked at her. "You know something don't you, Growler. What did you see that day? If only you could speak."

* * *

The very next day Emma knocked on Detective Crowley's door.

Detective Crowley stood up behind his desk. "Mrs. Kurtzler, what brings you here this fine day?"

"Hello, detective, it's about Frank."

He pointed to the chair opposite his desk and sat down. "Have a seat."

As soon as Emma sat down, she said, "I just thought I'd mention that there were two cups in the sink at Frank's *haus*."

"Yes, I noticed that. We had those cups tested and that's where we found the poison."

"So, he was poisoned?"

"Yes. Why are you only just telling me about the two cups now?"

Emma's heart started to race. The detective always made her feel as though she were guilty. "I only just remembered, only just this very morning."

"Have you been withholding any other information, Mrs. Kurtzler?"

Emma knew quite a bit, but thought she'd keep quiet

about Bob being there the very day of the murder. She was sure that Bob was no murderer. Bob was a little odd, but not a murderer. "Frank had ongoing disagreements with his neighbor, Thomas something or other. His last name escapes me for the moment."

"Yes, Thomas Graber; he's known to the police."

Emma tilted her head slightly to the side. "He is?"

Detective Crowley nodded. "Let's just say we've had dealings with him over other matters. What else have you found out?"

Emma was surprised that the Amish *mann,* Thomas Graber, would have had previous dealings with the police. "Did you find any prints on one of the cups that didn't belong to Frank? I mean the one that the other person might have drunk from?"

Crowley shook his head, then pushed back in his chair and let out a deep breath. Did the detective think that she was wasting his time?

"Mrs. Kurtzler, what's the real reason you've come here?"

"To tell you about the two cups. You said if I think of anything to let you know."

"Mrs. Kurtzler, Emma, I have to tell you that I do not need your help to solve a crime."

Emma gasped and jumped to her feet. "I'm tying to be of help. You told me to come to you if I thought of anything and that's what I'm doing."

The detective stayed seated and interlocked his fingers in front of him. "It's funny that I come across you again, in another murder case. Would that be fate or destiny?"

"I thought I might be able to help you, that's all. Seeing that I was the one who found him and I'm looking after his cat, and all." Emma knew she was not making any sense. Why did she mention Frank's cat? "I'll be going now, then." Emma walked straight out of Detective Crowley's office without saying goodbye to him.

She was glad that she did not mention the fact that Bob was there the day that Frank died. Bob was not one who was good with words, and he would never be able to explain himself to the police.

All the way home, Emma felt sick in the stomach. *Why is that detective so mean all the time? He always finds the very thing to say that would upset me.*

The next morning Emma called in on Wil. She knew it would be awkward to see him. She was not ready to speak of their disagreement.

Emma took a deep breath when he opened the door. "Can you give me the keys to Frank's *haus*? The ladies and I want to go and give it a *gut* clean."

"*Jah*, I've got a spare key. I'll fetch it for you. Do

you want to do that today?"

"Both Maureen and Silvie aren't working today, so today suits all of us."

Wil rubbed his chin. "Do you think it will be safe? They haven't found who did it, you know."

"*Jah*, it'll be safe with the five of us. Elsa-May and Ettie are going too."

Wil went around the corner into the kitchen and then came back with the key and handed it to her. "Emma, can we talk?"

"Not now, Wil."

The widows met at Frank's *haus* at noon, as they had planned. Maureen was to arrive as soon as she talked to Bob Pluver.

"What exactly are we looking for, Elsa-May?" Silvie asked.

"I don't really know. Tell me if you find anything, anything at all."

They were immediately disturbed by a knock on the door. Elsa-May opened the door to see Thomas Graber, Frank's next-door neighbor. "Hello, Thomas."

"Hello, Elsa-May. What are you ladies doing in here?" Thomas seemed jittery as he shifted his weight between his feet.

"We've come to give the place a *gut* cleaning," Emma said.

"Sad news about old Frank, wasn't it," Thomas said.

"*Jah,* that it was," Elsa-May said.

Thomas tipped his hat slightly back on his head. "Wonders me that anyone would have anything against old Frank and wish him harm."

Emma knew that the two men had many disagreements, the last one being about a fence that Thomas wanted to build between the two houses, but did that mean that Thomas would wish him harm? Surely not.

"Did you notice anything unusual in the last few days? Any strangers or visitors hanging around?" Elsa-May asked.

Thomas scratched his cheek. "Can't say so. Except the day he died, I heard some kind of ruckus. Someone was yelling I'm sure of it."

"I see, did you tell the police that?" Emma asked.

"*Jah*, there was a detective who questioned everyone in the street. I'm sure no one heard or saw anything, just me and the yelling."

"Okay, well thanks for popping by." Elsa-May tried to close the door and Thomas put his hand up against the door to hold it open. "Are you sure you ladies are supposed to be here?"

"Of course we are. Did you want to help us clean? We've got a spare scrubbing brush and soap. We could use some muscle power on the floors, especially the dried blood that's still there on the kitchen floor," Emma said.

"*Nee*, I've got to be somewhere soon." Thomas stuck his head through the door and had a good look around. "Carry on then."

When Elsa-May closed the door, Emma joined her in a fit of giggles. "What would you have done if he said he'd help with the dried blood only to find that there was none?"

"I was sure he wouldn't help," Emma said.

Elsa-May and Emma walked into the kitchen where Frank was found. "Found anything?" Elsa-May asked Ettie and Silvie, who were on their knees.

"*Jah*, a long strand of pale hair, could be gray or could be blonde, and a flake of red."

"Did you bag it?" Elsa-May asked.

"*Jah*." Silvie held up two plastic bags in her gloved hand.

"Wouldn't forensics have found everything?" Emma asked.

Elsa-May shook her head. "Not necessarily. Where's Maureen?"

"She's talking to Bob Pluver and then coming here, remember?" Ettie said.

"*Jah*, that's right. Now, Emma, let's think, what

would the murderer do, where would he have gone?"

"Seems that he went right through the entire *haus*."

At that moment, Maureen came through the front door. "Well, I have some news."

"We'll sit at the kitchen table," Elsa-May said.

When everyone was seated, Maureen began. "Bob said that he arrived here on the Thursday, at the time of his normal visit, and Frank seemed shaken by something. He had Bob drive him to the bank. Then Bob watched him as Frank walked to another bank. Then he had Bob drive him to a lawyer's office."

"Which lawyer?" Ettie said.

"I wrote it down, but I left it in the buggy. I think from memory it was Wagners & Sons, or something like that."

"Winters & Sons?" Silvie asked.

"*Jah*, that's the one."

Silvie sat up very straight. "I know George Winters. He comes into the bakery every single day."

"Okay, so seems like old Frank may have taken his money out of one bank and put it in another? Then he changed his will?" Elsa-May looked at all the other widows.

"He could have taken something out of a safe-deposit box," Maureen said.

"Did you ask Bob which banks he went to?"

Maureen shook her head.

"You'll have to go back and find out which banks. Not all have safe-deposit boxes and we need to know what he did at each bank."

"Couldn't the detective find that out?" Emma asked.

"*Ach, nee,* we can't tell him that Bob was here the day he died," Maureen said.

"Maureen's right, Emma. We don't want innocent people to get blamed for things they didn't do," Elsa-May said.

Emma nodded.

"Silvie, you will have to find out from George, what Frank was doing there that day, the day that he died."

"*Jah*, I'll do that today," Silvie said.

"Off you go now then," Elsa-May said.

Silvie looked down at her clothes. "I'm a mess. I'll have to go home and change first."

Elsa-May lowered her head and glared at Silvie. "Nonsense, you look fine. Go now."

"Okay," Silvie said as she headed quickly to the door.

"We'll wait for you; come straight back here," Elsa-May yelled after Silvie.

"Do we know anything of Frank's will?" Ettie asked.

"*Nee*, not that I've heard. Andrew was to have Wil let a realtor through to put a price on it, but he hasn't done that yet. Maybe that means that the *haus* is not left to Andrew? I'm not sure," Emma said.

"He only had Andrew and Clive and I'm sure he wouldn't have left something to one son and not the other," Maureen said.

"Maureen, you go back right now to Bob and find out what two banks Frank went to."

"Do I have to go back now? I don't want him to think that I like him," Maureen said.

Ettie giggled.

"That's the least of our problems, Maureen. Just go and find out those two things, hurry," Elsa-May said.

Maureen headed out the door with a most reluctant look on her face, which caused the three remaining widows to giggle.

"Poor Maureen," Emma said, "I do think that Bob is keen on her?"

"He'll be pleased to answer her questions then," Elsa-May said with a grin on her face.

"Well, come on girls; this place isn't going to clean itself," Ettie said.

Half an hour later, Maureen arrived back. After she told the widows which banks Frank went to, it was clear that he hadn't gone to the banks to take something out of a safe-deposit box, as neither bank had safe-deposit boxes.

"*Gut* work, Maureen," Elsa-May said.

"*Jah*, now I have to have dinner with him next week," Maureen said.

"He's the strong silent type, Maureen. There's nothing wrong with that boy and now he's inherited his *daed's* business, he's quite a catch," Ettie said with a twinkle in her eye.

"I hear a buggy, must be Silvie back," Emma said.

A minute later, Silvie burst through the door, quite breathless. "Phew, it took me a while and two cups of coffee, but old Mr. Winters told me that Frank insisted on changing his will there and then, so his 'useless' sons would get nothing."

Elsa-May leaned forward and asked, "So who did he leave his money to?"

"Bob, Bob Pluver. And Bob's to see that Growler is looked after."

Emma covered her mouth. "Bob."

Elsa-May said, "That means that Bob is now our prime suspect. That's not *gut*. It means that we can't listen to what he told us. If he killed Frank, he could've made up the entire thing he told Maureen."

"He was right about going to the lawyer, though," Maureen said. "He didn't lie about that."

"*Jah*, That's right, Maureen." Ettie laughed. "But that was to his advantage to know where the most recent will was kept."

Maureen shook her head. "I don't believe that he did it."

"Neither do I, but he does move to front place as far as the suspects are concerned," Elsa-May said.

"Are you going to tell the detective, Elsa-May?" Maureen said.

Elsa-May narrowed her eyes. "I don't know. I think we should sit on the information for now."

The widows had been silent for a moment, before Ettie asked, "You've got the cat, haven't you, Emma?"

"I'm afraid so. He just ignores me all the time; I don't know how the old man got so attached to him. He just sleeps, eats, and he's taken over the whole *haus*."

"You must look after him well, Emma. That was Frank's wish," Silvie said.

"I will. He already has the run of the *haus*." Emma gave a little giggle; she was not brave enough to tell the widows that the cat slept on her bed. They would consider her far too soft in the head.

"Why would Frank suddenly decide to leave all his money to Bob on that very day? What had him so shaken?" Elsa-May drummed her fingertips onto her chin. "Ettie, go out to the buggy and get me my writing pad."

Ettie came back into the *haus* within moments with a pen and Elsa-May's writing pad.

Elsa-May began writing. "Suspects? We have the old man next door, the two sons and Bob."

"*Nee*, not Bob," Maureen said.

Elsa-May glanced up at Maureen and then set her eyes once more to her writing pad. "As I was saying, Bob, and who else would have had something to gain from the man's death?"

"When Andrew and his girlfriend were here the other day, he mentioned something; he thought his *daed* had in a safe-deposit box somewhere," Emma said.

Elsa-May pushed out her lips. "Maybe he did have something in a safe-deposit box somewhere. Did we find a key anywhere?" The widows all shook their heads. "Perhaps the detective found a key. I'll pay him a visit and give him what we found and ask him a few questions."

Elsa-May scribbled down a few more things on to her writing pad. "Let's re-cap. Frank was upset by something –most likely to do with his sons, because he had Bob drive him to town where he went to two banks and then changed his will at the solicitor's. And that's only if Bob was telling Maureen the truth."

"He was, I'm sure of it," Maureen said.

"Did Bob come into Frank's *haus* on the Thursday, the day that Frank died?" Silvie asked.

"He said that he didn't," Maureen said. "He had to

go back to work."

"So we can't say at what time Frank's home was broken into and wrecked. Frank was upset, went to banks, solicitor, back home, and that's all we know until Emma came later in the day and found him poisoned on the floor," Elsa-May said as she studied her writing pad.

"*Jah*, seems to be all we know so far," Ettie said. "His boys had to have been upset with him because he changed his will. That part is obvious."

"Would one of his sons have killed him if Frank told them what he'd done about changing the will?" Emma asked.

"*Nee*, because then he'd never be alive to change the will back," Elsa-May said. "It's pointing more and more to Bob."

"Can't we rule out the man next door? It's a bit weird to think someone could kill someone over just a fence," Silvie said.

"Ahh, but it's never just a fence. The fence could be the last straw, as the expression goes; the last straw that broke the camel's back. We can't rule anyone out."

Chapter 8

Be kindly affectioned one to another with brotherly love; in honour preferring one another; Not slothful in business; fervent in spirit; serving the Lord; Rejoicing in hope; patient in tribulation; continuing instant in prayer; Distributing to the necessity of saints; given to hospitality.
Romans 12:10-13

It was on the Saturday after the funeral that Silvie heard a knock at her door. She opened it to see her younger *schweschder*, Sabrina, with a suitcase in her hand. Silvie looked up the road to see a taxi driving away. "Sabrina, what are you doing here?"

Sabrina pushed past Silvie into the *haus*. "*Mamm* sent me."

"She did? How did you get here?"

"I came on the Greyhound." Sabrina put her bag down just inside the door and took off her coat.

Silvie took her coat from her. "I don't mean to sound rude, but why are you here?"

"*Mamm* heard that you were very friendly with an *Englischer* at a funeral."

Silvie was surprised how fast news traveled. "There is a man, but he's staying in the community because he wants to become Amish, that's all. There's nothing going on with me and him."

"Really?" Sabrina raised an eyebrow and stared at Silvie. It reminded Silvie of how her *mudder* had always stared at her when she'd done something wrong. Silvie's *mudder* was a dominating force and Silvie had escaped that domination when she married John. At that moment, Silvie realized that getting away from her *mudder* might have been a major factor in her decision to marry John.

"Why do you come to my *haus* and question me? I'm a grown woman and can do as I please," Silvie said as she hung up Sabrina's coat.

"Do what you want." Sabrina laughed. "I just had to get away for a while and this was a *gut* excuse. Besides, it'll give me a chance to meet the *menner* in the community. Is there anyone who might suit me?"

Silvie reached for Sabrina's suitcase. "I'll take this up to the spare room. Come, I'll show you where it is."

"Silvie, you didn't answer me. There are no *menner* for me in Ohio so I'm hoping there might be someone here for me. You'd like to have a *schweschder* here, wouldn't you? It must be lonely out here all by yourself."

Her *schweschder* or for that matter, any member of her *familye* staying in Lancaster County, was far less than an ideal situation for Silvie. "It's the second Sunday tomorrow so there'll be a meeting; come see for yourself."

Sabrina clapped her hands together. "Goodie. You don't mind me staying a while, do you?"

"Of course not," Silvie said as she heaved the heavy suitcase onto the bed. "I'll be pleased of the company." Silvie wondered who there might be for Sabrina. "There are a few single *menner* you might like."

"*Ach*, I can't wait for tomorrow to see for myself."

"*Mamm* sent you to spy on me?"

"She sent me to make sure that you don't make a mistake. She was worried when she heard about the *Englischer*." Sabrina sat down heavily on the other side of the bed. "Who is he, the *Englischer*?"

"No one important. Just someone who might become Amish soon, that's all, but I'm a grown woman and can make my own choices; I wish *mamm* would realize that. Apparently, I'm not far enough away from her." Silvie wondered who it was who reported back to her *mudder*.

"Silvie, that's a terrible thing to say. *Mamm* would be so upset to hear you say a thing like that about her."

Silvie laughed. "You only just said that you needed

to get away too."

"I didn't say it was because of *mamm*. I mind what I say." Sabrina pouted.

"Okay, then I'll mind what I say as well. You get settled, unpack your clothes and you can help me with the chores."

"Chores? I'm a guest. I don't want to do any chores; I have to do chores at home."

Silvie shook a finger at Sabrina. "If you stay here, you'll be doing chores."

Sabrina pouted once more. "If I'd known that, I would not have come."

Silvie turned and walked toward the bedroom door. "If you want to stay with me, you have to do chores. I'll give you fifteen minutes to unpack." Silvie walked out of the bedroom pleased with herself. If her *mudder* had sent Sabrina to spy on her, she had to turn things to her advantage in the best way that she could.

As Silvie finished washing the dishes, she looked out the window and remembered her prayer of just days ago. She shared with *Gott* that she did not want to be alone. Was this *Gott's* answer, to send her Sabrina? She meant she wanted a *mann* in her life, not her spoiled *schweschder* to come and stay with her. She would have to be more specific with her prayers in the future.

Chapter 9

*For as the body without the spirit/breath is dead,
so faith without works is dead also.*
James 2:26

Emma drove herself to the Sunday meeting rather than go with Maureen or Wil. Sometimes she liked to be alone driving to the gathering together and back home.

Walking toward the group, she saw Silvie and was sure that the woman next to her had to be Silvie's *schweschder*. She had the same fine features and the same delicate coloring with the blonde hair and the blue eyes.

Silvie looked up, caught her eye and walked over to her with her arm looped through her *schweschder's*. "Emma, this is Sabrina, my *schweschder*."

"Hello, Sabrina." Up close the girl was even more beautiful than Silvie.

"Nice to meet you, Emma."

Emma noticed that Sabrina was hardly paying her any attention as her eyes darted to and fro over the crowd. It was clear to Emma that Sabrina was single and looking for a husband. Most young girls of her age thought of little else. "I guess you're from Ohio too, Sabrina?"

"*Jah*, I don't know how long I'm staying yet, maybe just a week or so."

Sabrina and Silvie sat with Maureen and Emma during the service.

When the meal was being served afterward, Silvie pulled Emma aside. "*Mamm* sent her to spy on me because she heard that I was sweet on an *Englischer*."

"Really? I guessed that she was looking for a husband."

"*Jah*, that too."

Emma laughed, and they both turned to look at Sabrina only to see her approach Wil. "*Ach*, look she's gone over to Wil. Emma, you have to stop her."

Emma scoffed. "I'm not concerned. Wil had plenty of time to find someone else besides me; he's never been interested in anyone else."

Silvie frowned. "You're very confident, Emma."

Emma was not confident at all, not after the argument they had. "We've talked of marriage."

"You haven't said 'yes' though, have you?"

"*Nee*, but we have an understanding. He knows it's too soon for me to say 'yes.'"

Although Emma knew that Wil loved her, Silvie's words began to concern her. "Let's go closer to hear what they are talking about," Emma said.

Wil immediately looked up as they approached. "Ahh, Silvie you have a delightful *schweschder.*"

Silvie smiled and looked at Emma.

"Emma, have you met Sabrina?"

Emma noticed that as Wil spoke he shifted his weight from one foot to another as if he was nervous.

"*Jah*, we met earlier." Emma looked at Sabrina and was sure that she looked disappointed that her talk with Wil had been interrupted. Could Sabrina see Wil as a potential husband even though she was only eighteen and he was in his thirties? Surely not.

"Sabrina's interested in my inventions."

Emma raised her eyebrows. She did not see how anyone could be interested in Wil's inventions. How did they come to speak of his inventions so quickly? "Is she?"

"*Jah*, I do a little fiddling with inventions myself." Sabrina was certainly more animated in her conversation when there was a man around.

"Such as?" Emma asked, wondering if Sabrina would dare to make up such a thing.

"*Mamm* has a gas powered iron and I've made it into a battery powered iron by fitting it with a battery pack that I made myself."

Emma laughed and before she could stop herself,

she said, "What would be the use of that?"

Wil stared at her and Emma knew that he sensed something was not right with her. Did Wil know that she was a little jealous of this new girl?

Sabrina tilted her chin high. "Well, *mamm* liked it. She found it more convenient."

"*Jah*, I'm sure it's got many convenient uses." Emma tried to sound sincere to cover her previous cruel outburst.

Sabrina ignored Emma's words and said, "Why don't you show me some of your inventions, Wil?"

"Of course, have Silvie bring you for dinner one night this week. That'll be okay, won't it, Silvie?"

Silvie smiled. "*Jah*, we could come tomorrow night."

"Tomorrow it is then."

"Come on, Sabrina." Silvie linked her arm through Sabrina's. "I've got some people I want you to meet. Excuse us, Wil, Emma." Silvie pulled Sabrina away, leaving Wil and Emma alone.

"You'll come to dinner on tomorrow too, of course?" Wil asked Emma.

"Do you want me to?" Emma asked.

"Of course, all my dinner invitations include you."

Emma folded her arms and looked into the distance. She had never experienced the emotion of jealousy, but now she knew what it was. She was annoyed at

Sabrina for speaking to Wil and not just speaking, she was flirting with him. Outrageously flirting and she even invited herself to his *haus*. The sheer nerve of the woman. "Don't you know that Sabrina is attracted to you? She's only here from Ohio to look for a husband."

"That's a little harsh, Emma. You've only just met the girl. You were also rude to her."

Emma's mouth fell open at Wil's words. "I was not."

Wil rubbed the back of his neck. "You've never understood about my inventions have you?"

"What do you mean? I do understand about your inventions."

"When someone invents something, it's important to them. You have never shown any interest in my inventions - ever." Wil nodded his head in a definite manner as he spoke.

Emma remained silent; she was not the slightest bit interested in his senseless tinkering with useless objects, and why should she be? They were a sheer waste of *Gott's* time. Why couldn't Wil see that for himself?

Wil continued, "Think of it like your needlework. You spend hours on your needlework and show me what you've done and I show interest in your work – the fine stitches, the different colors. But, if I try and speak about my inventions or try to show you, you just don't pay any mind. You make no effort to even pretend to have a tiny piece of curiosity."

Emma looked up at Wil. He was scolding her. He had never spoken crossly like that to her before.

Wil continued, "You even told that girl that her invention was of no use. How would you feel if someone told you your needlework was of no use to anybody?"

Emma jutted out her bottom lip as she thought of Sabrina's invention. "Well, I think the battery iron was silly and I do think it's of no use. I have to be truthful." Couldn't Wil see that a battery pack on an iron was pointless when a gas-powered iron would've done the same thing? Why was he defending the girl, because she was pretty and young?

"What use is your needlework? What use is it to anybody?"

Emma scoffed. "It's hardly the same thing, Wil."

"It might not be the same thing, but it's about people's feelings. Think about other people for once, Emma." Wil put his hands on his hips and his eyes flashed with disappointment.

"Are you saying that I'm selfish?" Emma asked.

Wil slowly nodded his head. "*Jah*, something like that. If you'll excuse me, I see someone I need to speak to." Wil walked away from Emma with long, fast strides.

Emma's eyes filled with tears. Never had he spoken to her like that. Wil had been her rock ever since Levi had died. Wil was her best friend and now he had said mean things to her and for no reason.

Feeling all alone in the world, Emma walked directly to her buggy, hoping that no one would see her in tears. She drove all the way home with tears brimming in her eyes. She was pleased that she had decided to drive there alone that day.

Was she selfish? Could Wil be right? No one else had ever called her selfish.

She opened her front door, lay down on the couch, closed her eyes and thought on Wil's words. He was as *gut* as saying that she was selfish for not showing interest in his silly inventions. She was sick on the tummy. It was true she never showed any interest but he had never been angry about it before, not 'til she hadn't shown any interest in Sabrina's useless invention. Maybe Wil was sweet on Sabrina. Could it be more than a coincidence that he picked a fight with her straight after he met the young and pretty Sabrina?

No one had ever said that needlework was a waste of time. *At least I have something to show for all my time*, Emma thought of her sewing.

Emma went into the kitchen to make herself

something to eat. Growler was finishing the last of the meat she had put out for him that morning. "Hello, Growler." As usual, Growler ignored her and kept eating. She leaned over and stroked his gray, silver fur until he purred.

She walked past Growler into the utility room and spied some chocolates and decided that she needed something to cheer herself up. Emma took the chocolates back to the lounge and covered herself with a blanket. As the chocolate melted in her mouth, she thought of more than a few times that Wil had tried to show her what he was working on. Sometimes she would laugh, or scoff and sometimes she would say she'd look later, but never did. Perhaps she should show interest in what he did with his time, but couldn't he see that his inventions were useless? Even Levi had said that they were a waste of time.

Maybe she wasn't a match with Wil as she had thought. Maybe loneliness was the only factor that had driven her to find comfort and companionship with Wil.

Chapter 10

And the multitude of them that believed were of one heart and of one soul: neither said any of them that ought of the things which he possessed was his own; but they had all things common.
Acts 4:32

Typically Emma would have offered to cook when Wil had guests but considering their cross words of late, Emma thought she would leave Wil to cook on his own. She thought by doing so he would appreciate her more and not speak to her so meanly in the future.

She arrived at Wil's *haus* at 6 p.m. only to find that Silvie was already there so she assumed that Sabrina would be as well.

Silvie and Bailey were talking on the porch on two large wooden chairs. "Hello, Emma," Silvie said.

"Hello, you two. Where are Wil and Sabrina?"

"Sabrina's helping Wil in the kitchen."

The nerve of the girl; she's trying to step right into my shoes. Emma was angry with herself for not helping Wil as she usually did. Because of her pride and selfishness, she had unknowingly opened a way for Sabrina to work her way into Wil's heart.

Emma looked down at the apple pie in her hands. "I'll be back in a minute. I'll just take the apple pie into the kitchen." Was she going to be the odd one out tonight? Silvie and Bailey were attracted to each other and Wil and Sabrina had their inventions to chat about. Emma walked quickly into the kitchen. "I brought apple pie."

"*Denke*, Emma. I love your apple pie."

"I know. I made it especially for you." Emma tried to make it sound as though they were a couple in front of Sabrina. "Hello, Sabrina. *Denke* for helping Wil; I usually help him with the cooking, but I was busy with other things today."

"Hello, Emma. I couldn't see Wil do all the cooking himself. He needs a *fraa* to look after him." Sabrina shot an adoring look at Wil, which annoyed Emma greatly.

Wil and she were courting, didn't Sabrina know that; hadn't Silvie told her to keep away from him?

When Wil remained silent, Emma walked out of the kitchen and sat out on the porch with Bailey and Silvie. They stopped speaking when she approached.

"How are you going with things, Bailey?" Emma asked.

"Fine, *denke*, Emma. I'm learning a lot and taking it all in. I'll be Amish in no time."

"That's *gut*." Trying not to clench her mouth, Emma asked, "Silvie, how long is Sabrina staying with you?"

"I don't know. She's enjoying a little freedom away from *mamm*."

That was the answer that Emma did not want to hear. She had no one to discipline her and she was set loose on the *menner* in the community, in particular Wil.

Wil and Sabrina came through the front door. "I'm just going to show Sabrina some of my inventions in the barn. Do you want to come with us, Emma?"

"*Jah*, I'll go and have a look." Emma considered that she was in a difficult position. While she was glad that Wil asked her, she did not want to appear to Sabrina as though she was jealous of her. She would also have to leave Bailey and Silvie alone with each other.

While Wil showed Sabrina and Emma all the things he had invented, Sabrina made all the appropriate oohs and ahhhs while Emma found it difficult to muster the appropriate enthusiasm.

The whole night Emma felt totally out of sorts. Sabrina took over her role as hostess and Emma spent the night forcing a smile on her face.

Once everyone had gone, Emma turned to Wil. "I'd better get going too."

"*Nee*, wait, Emma. I'm sorry for what I said to you on Sunday. It was mean."

"You were right, Wil. I've been so consumed with myself and feeling sorry for what happened to me that I haven't been aware of other people's needs. Well, your needs."

Wil said, "I'll walk you home."

Although they had both apologized to one another, something had changed. Emma knew in her heart that things between them were not the same.

* * *

The tension between Wil and Emma played on her mind so much that Emma knew she had to have a straight talk with Wil about it. The next morning Emma stopped in on Wil on her way to town. "Are you there, Wil?"

Wil came to the door with a coffee cup in his hands. "Emma, come in."

"How about we sit out here, in the morning sun?"

"Okay, would you like a *kaffe*?"

"*Nee*, I just had one at home. Wil, I feel things between us are different."

Wil smiled. *"Are they?"*

"If something's important to you, I will try and understand why it interests you."

Wil reached out and took hold of Emma's hand. "Let's not speak of it again. We said all we needed to say last night."

"Okay," Emma said.

"Let's just enjoy this beautiful sunny day before the cold weather sets in."

Emma took a deep breath and let it out slowly while she enjoyed the sunlight on her face. She was happy not to speak of things that they would disagree on.

"Have you heard the latest about Frank?" Emma tried to change the subject.

"*Nee*, what's happened?" Wil asked.

"Oh, I know nothing. I wondered if you'd heard anything. It was a little difficult to talk last night with all the people around."

"*Nee*, I've heard of nothing. They are trying to locate Frank's will and that's all I know," Wil said.

Emma bit her lip. She had to keep quiet about the will since she wasn't supposed to know about the will. "Ettie did a bit of digging about Frank's past before he came to the community. Anyway, he was an auctioneer and Ettie seems to think that he might have some paintings hidden away somewhere." Emma giggled nervously knowing that she should not have talked about things that came out of the widows' meeting.

Wil, sprung to his feet. "Emma, I completely forgot about the paintings."

Emma rose to her feet. "What paintings? Wil, what do you mean?"

"It was years ago; that's why I forgot about them. One day Frank brought some paintings to me. That was just after his *fraa*, Sally, died and before he moved into the smaller *haus.*"

"Go on."

"He said if anything should happen to him, I'm to give them to his boys."

"Where are the paintings now?" Emma asked.

"I wrapped them in brown paper and a large blanket and put them up in the roof."

"Go and see if they're still there, but don't tell Bailey what you're doing."

"Okay, I'll be back soon. I think Bailey's out with Silvie anyway."

"*Gut*. Wait, I'll come with you."

The two of them walked quickly into Wil's *haus.* Wil had a ladder already at the back door as he'd been working on his roof. He climbed the ladder and pushed aside the entry into the ceiling. "Hand me that kerosene lamp, would you?"

Emma lit the lamp and handed it to him.

"*Jah,* seems they're still here."

"That's far enough. Both of you stay where you are."

Emma held her stomach at the sight of Bailey Abler with a gun in his hand. Wil ducked his head back into the room.

Bailey took a step closer. "Emma, stay where you are and put your hands in the air. Wil, get the paintings and come down the ladder very, very slowly."

Emma obeyed him and raised her hands above her head. Once Wil got to the bottom of the ladder he placed the paintings still wrapped in a blanket onto the floor.

"What is the meaning of this, Bailey? What are you doing pointing a gun at us?"

"I need to ask you, Wil, what are you doing with stolen art work?" Bailey asked.

"Stolen? Frank asked me to take care of them. Emma has just jogged my memory of them. He placed them in my care years ago and never mentioned them to me again." As Bailey slowly walked closer, Wil asked, "Who are they stolen from? Or do you think that we stole them?"

Emma was relieved to hear the sound of a buggy stopping outside the *haus*. Emma glanced at Bailey's startled face. Surely he couldn't shoot everyone. Emma lowered her hands.

"Bailey, what are you doing?"

Emma knew that the booming voice belonged to Elsa-May. Behind Elsa-May she saw Ettie and Maureen.

Bailey addressed Elsa-May. "I just found that these two are in possession of stolen paintings."

"Nonsense." Elsa-May pushed the gun in his hand down.

Emma quickly told Elsa-May, "Wil remembered that Frank had given him the paintings to look after. How did you know to come here?"

"We were coming to visit you when we saw your buggy here at Wil's place." Elsa-May ignored Bailey and walked right past him. "Did you say paintings? Well, let's unwrap them and take a look."

Bailey put his hand agitatedly to his forehead. "Aunt Em, you can't just walk into my investigation like this."

Elsa-May swung around to Bailey. "Wil, Emma, meet my and Ettie's nephew, Bailey Rivers. He's a detective."

Emma gasped and Wil said, "You're Elsa-May and Ettie's nephew?" Emma was relieved that he was not a thief or a murderer.

Bailey nodded. "Well, great nephew, really."

"So you don't want to join the Amish? Your name's not Bailey Abler?" Wil asked.

"Sorry to do that to you, Wil. I'm Bailey Rivers. You've been very kind to me, showing me how everything works, the traditions and the customs."

"This is such a shock." Emma put her hands to her head.

"I think the person you should apologize to should

be Silvie," Wil said with deep furrows in his brow. "Does the bishop know of this deception?"

Bailey lowered his head. "The bishop knew from the start."

Wil shook his head.

"I'm afraid I'm the one who organized things for Bailey to be here, Wil," Elsa-May said, "Now, let's have a look at these paintings."

Elsa-May and Bailey carefully unwrapped the paintings while Wil and the others looked on.

There were three small paintings. "This one looks to be a Chagall, that one is by Otto Dix and I don't know who that one was painted by, but it looks to be a 16th century painting." Elsa-May rose to her feet. "You see, a lot of art went missing in World War Two from Germany."

"How do you know all these things, Elsa-May?" Emma asked.

Elsa-May flung a hand in the air. "I studied art history in college."

"You went to college?" Maureen asked.

Elsa-May smiled and nodded.

Emma's head felt as though it was spinning with all the surprises. "So Frank was murdered for these paintings? They don't look like they're worth much at all," Emma said.

"We could be looking at millions, Emma," Elsa-May said.

Emma's hand flew to her mouth. "Millions?"

"What have you found out, Aunt Em?" Bailey asked.

Emma knew she should be concentrating on the paintings, but all she could think of was how devastated Silvie would be.

"Well, you obviously knew about Frank's father's art dealings and you knew that he'd have these paintings hidden somewhere," Elsa-May said.

"Yes, I've been on the trail of the paintings for a long time. Funny that they should bring me here to the same community where you are," Bailey said.

"And the same community that Silvie's in," Emma said, hoping he would see that she was cranky with him for leading her dear friend up the garden path.

"If only you'd come a little earlier, you could have saved old Frank from being murdered," Wil said.

"Do any of you have any idea who could have done it?" Bailey asked.

"Yes, that was my question," Detective Crowley said as he walked through the door. He glanced at the three paintings on the floor. "So you've found the paintings, Rivers?"

"Yes, seems that the old man gave them to Wil to look after, and Wil's only just remembered about it."

The detective raised his eyebrows. "How convenient."

"Look here, what are you implying?" Wil said with a raised voice.

"I can vouch for Wil and Emma, Detective. They're just innocent bystanders in all this," Elsa-May said. It appeared that Elsa-May had a fair amount of influence over the detective.

Was the detective also a relative of Elsa-May's and Ettie's? Emma wondered.

"Well, if neither of them did it, who killed Frank?" Crowley asked.

"I don't know, but I will have to take these paintings and have them verified. I'll call for a photographer first and have them catalogued before I move them." He looked at Detective Crowley. "I should also probably have them dusted for prints."

"Yes, if it's not too late," he said looking at Elsa-May and Wil.

"I was careful only to touch the corners of the frames," Elsa-May said.

"I only touched them years ago," Wil said.

Emma remained silent until the detective stared at her. "Oh, I haven't touched them at all."

"I'll get the fingerprint team down here." Detective Crowley walked out the door while pushing buttons on his cell phone.

"They promised me full co-operation," Bailey said nodding his head to Crowley.

"What prints would you expect since the person looking for them at Frank's *haus* didn't find them? It wouldn't have their prints on them," Elsa-May said.

"I know; it's just routine. We have to do things properly." Bailey lowered his voice, "Especially with Crowley breathing down my neck. I can't do anything unless it's completely by the book."

Chapter 11

And on the seventh day God ended his work which he had made; and he rested on the seventh day from all his work which he had made.
And God blessed the seventh day, and sanctified it: because that in it he had rested from all his work which God created and made.
Genesis 2:2-3

"Detective, have you found anything out?" Elsa-May asked him when the detective came back inside the *haus* after speaking on his cell.

"It so happens that we have new information from the son, Andrew. He admitted to being there that morning. Andrew had fallen on hard times and thought his father had something of great value that he might be able to sell. His father denied having anything at all and a shouting match broke out."

"Must have been these paintings that Frank was protecting," Wil said.

The detective took a step forward. "Well, no one will get them since they're stolen."

"Not so fast." Bailey held up each painting and took a good look at them. "I dare say that these aren't any of the paintings I was chasing. Two of them are very similar. These might very well be the real deal."

"What do you mean, the real deal?" Detective Crowley asked him.

"They might not be stolen." Bailey carefully looked at the back of the paintings with gloved hands. "Just as I hoped. It appears something is stuck to the back of each painting; no doubt it would be the receipts and authentication. I think we will find that these aren't stolen."

"So the sons will come into an inheritance?" Maureen asked as if she was disappointed.

"Appears so," Bailey said.

The sound of a car screeching to a halt made everyone's heads turn toward Wil's front door. Wil went outside the *haus* to greet Andrew, Frank's son.

"Wil, I've just been to the bank and all the money was cleaned out of dad's account, all of it."

Wil jerked his head back. "Did they say when the money was taken out?"

"The day he died. The very day he died, all the money gone." Andrew put a hand on Wil to steady himself and looked as though he was about to collapse.

"Detective Crowley is here. Come inside." Wil helped Andrew into the *haus*.

Wil told Crowley what Andrew had just told him,

while Andrew sat breathing heavily on the couch with his hand on his chest.

Detective Crowley sat opposite Andrew and scratched in his notebook. "Did anyone at the bank see if he was accompanied by anyone?"

Andrew shook his head. "They didn't say."

"Should be on their CCTV. I'll check into it."

Wil said, "Andrew, these are your *daed's* paintings. He told me if anything should happen to him to give them to you and Clive. I'm sorry, but I only just remembered them."

Andrew hurried over to the paintings and sank to his knees. "This must be what he told us about. Something of tremendous value for us boys."

Bailey stepped forward. "You can't touch them. We need to have them fingerprinted and authenticated to check that they aren't stolen first. I'll need to take them for a while."

"My *daed* was a man of *Gott*. He would never steal," Andrew said.

"I don't mean to offend you. I'm Detective Bailey Rivers."

"What's going on here? Why would you think that they were stolen?" Andrew asked. When Wil told him about Bailey being on the trail of stolen paintings, Andrew asked Bailey, "How long will you have to take them for?"

"Three days, I've got someone coming in from Chicago. Hopefully, they'll be here tomorrow so we can get this thing wrapped up. I've been chasing some stolen paintings, but I'm sure I'm on the wrong trail with these ones."

"Do what you need to do. I'm confident that they're not stolen," Andrew said.

"Andrew, what's keeping you?" Andrew's girlfriend called out to him from the doorway. "I'm coming, Lacey, and I've got some good news."

Emma noticed that Lacey had long blonde hair and today her long nails were pink, but the day Emma met her they were red. An alarm bell went off in Emma's head, the long strand of hair, the red flake, which could've been a piece of red nail polish. Emma looked up at Elsa-May and by the look on her face Emma knew that she was thinking the same thing.

While Andrew was showing the girlfriend the paintings, Elsa-May pulled the detective aside and whispered in his ear.

The detective stood behind the girl and asked, "Tell me, Lacey, were you at Frank's *haus* the day that he died?"

"No, she wasn't there. She waited in the car for me," Andrew answered for her.

"I'm asking this young lady, not you, sir." The detective looked back at Lacey. "Well, young lady?"

"No, like he said, I was in the car."

"In that case you wouldn't mind giving me a DNA sample would you?"

Lacey's face stiffened. "No, I'm not going to waste my time with such a thing." Lacey looked at Andrew. "Tell them, Andrew."

"How long will it take, detective?" Andrew adjusted his trousers. "We've got lunch reservations."

"I'll have someone here in ten minutes." The detective stepped outside and made a call on his cell phone.

"Is Lacey a suspect?" Andrew asked when the detective came back inside.

"Not especially, but everyone is giving DNA samples and we haven't got one from her yet. I could get a warrant, if need be."

Andrew slumped into the couch and wiped the sweat off his forehead. "We can wait ten minutes. You don't mind if we inconvenience you for ten more minutes do you, Wil?" Andrew asked.

"*Nee*, of course not."

"I'll make us some tea," Emma said and hurried to the kitchen with Elsa-May close behind her.

"What do you think?" Elsa-May whispered to Emma.

"She does have the long, pale hair and that red flake we found could be that nail varnish she was wearing," Emma whispered back. "She was after the thing of value that old Frank had spoken of. She could have come back after Andrew ransacked the place and tried to get it out of the old man, where the valuables were."

"*Jah*, that makes sense because he was poisoned with a lethal dose of sodium pentothal." On seeing the blank look on Emma's face, Elsa-May said, "Truth serum."

"When did you find that out?"

"Crowley told me as soon as he found out. I didn't put two and two together at the time. Now, it makes sense."

"What about all his money disappearing from the bank? Do you think Bob could've had anything to do with it?" Emma asked.

"I'd hate to think so. I don't think Bob would've done such a thing. He's always been honest in his dealings," Elsa-May said.

When they brought the tea into the living room, Andrew and the detective were speaking to each other on the couch.

"I've admitted to looking through the house, but I didn't kill him and I didn't ransack the place," Andrew said.

The detective said, "You've told the police all this in

your statement, haven't you?"

Andrew nodded.

The detective continued, "Did you see Bob Pluver?"

"I was parked up the road with Lacey later that day and we saw him go past in the buggy with Bob Pluver."

"Then where did you go?" the detective asked.

"Lacey had a hair appointment..."

Lacey interrupted as she bounded to her feet. "I don't want to wait for the DNA people. I already told you that I've never been to the *haus*."

"I could get a warrant; it'll only take me a couple of hours." The detective's tone was firm.

Lacey walked toward the door. "Come on, Andrew. Let's go."

"We should just wait and get it over with, Lacey. He said he could get a warrant and then you'll just have to go to the bother of doing it another time."

Lacey's voice rose. "I said that I don't want to stay, Andrew."

Andrew looked shocked as if he had never heard Lacey raise her voice. "Whatever's gotten into you, just stay? It won't take long."

"We found some hair and some other material we can identify. The hair was long and blonde. Is there anything you'd like to tell me, Lacey? We can also check with the hairdresser to see if you kept that appointment."

Lacey looked at the floor. "It was an accident. I didn't mean to kill him. I just wanted him to tell me where the valuables were. I gave him truth serum, only a bit. He must've had an allergic reaction or something."

Andrew jumped to his feet. "You did what?"

Lacey began to cry and ran to Andrew and put her head on his shoulder. "I'm sorry. I'm sorry. I didn't give him much at all."

Andrew whispered to her. "Don't say anything until we get a lawyer."

"Where did you get the sodium pentothal from?" The detective asked.

Lacey shrugged and raised her head slightly. "I'm not saying any else."

"One more thing I should tell you, Andrew." Detective Crowley said.

"And what's that?" Andrew asked.

"The will you have in your possession has been superseded. He wrote a new will the day that he died. I'm afraid that you and your brother are no longer the benefactors."

"No. It must be a fake will. It can't be real."

"He had a lawyer witness it. I can assure you it is real." Detective Crowley said.

Lacey jumped back from Andrew. "You idiot,

Andrew. Can't you do anything right?"

"Shut up, Lacey. Clive and I will contest it. Who's the benefactor?"

"Bob Pluver is the sole benefactor. I wouldn't waste your time or your money contesting anything, not after you both terrorized the old man and finally killed him."

Lacey hurried to the door. "Let's go Andrew."

The detective stepped in front of her. "Lacey, you have to come with me."

Sirens sounded and everyone stayed still. Seconds later, two police officers ran into the house.

Emma remembered she saw the detective on his phone minutes before and realized he had called for backup.

The detective pointed to Lacey as he spoke to the officers. "You can take this one back to the station."

As the officers led Lacey away, Andrew said, "I'll follow them in my car, sweetie."

The detective sat down.

"Tea?" Elsa-May said as she held up the teapot.

The detective grunted. "I'll need something stronger than tea, but I suppose tea will do for now."

"Did I hear you right? Bob inherited everything?" Emma asked.

"It appears that Bob was preparing to have the old man move into a small *haus* that he'd built on to his own. He called it a *daadi haus*. You Amish look after your own, I'm told." He smirked at Emma.

Emma smiled back. "That's right; we do."

Wil said, "His sons hadn't visited him in years so I don't see that they would've taken him in when he got too feeble to look after himself. Bob was doing a *gut* thing."

"I knew Bob wouldn't have done anything bad," Maureen said.

Emma signaled to Bailey to meet her in the kitchen.

"Bailey, have you thought of how upset Silvie will be when she knows that this was all not real – you intending to join the community?"

"Yes, I have and it's upset me from the start. I feel such a pull toward her that I couldn't bring myself to stay away from her."

Emma was annoyed with Bailey for pursuing a relationship with Silvie in the first place when he knew that he would not be staying. "She took quite a liking to you and she has never shown interest in any other man since her husband died."

"I'll go straight to her place and tell her, as soon as I can. I'm sorry to deceive you and Wil too, but that's the nature of my business, I guess."

Emma folded her arms. "Maybe you should get into a different business then."

Bailey nodded. "Excuse me, I'll have to arrange to take the paintings away."

"Once again, Elsa-May, thank you for your assistance," the detective said then quickly drank the rest of his tea. "I must be going – paperwork."

"Detective, I must ask. Was the hair that we found useable for the DNA test, did it have the root follicle attached?"

Detective Crowley grinned, "They weren't able to use it, but we don't need it now that we have a confession."

* * *

Silvie sat at the kitchen table and took a moment to enjoy the peace and quiet in the *haus* now that Sabrina had taken the buggy into town. A car pulling up in her driveway disturbed her peace. As she opened her front door, she saw Bailey getting out of a car.

"Bailey, why are you driving a car?"

Bailey hurried toward her. "Silvie, can we speak inside?"

"*Jah*, of course."

Bailey led her by the hand to her couch, sat her down, and said, "I've a lot of things to tell you. You just missed all the action at Wil's *haus*."

"I did? What happened?"

He filled Silvie in on what happened with the

paintings, Lacey's confession and Bob inheriting Frank's estate.

Bailey reached for Silvie's hand and held it in his. "I've always been fascinated by the Amish. I'm a Christian and I have admired the faith and strength of the Amish for a long time."

"What are you trying to say? Have you changed your mind about joining us?"

"I'm afraid I've deceived you. I am a detective – undercover, and I've been on the trail of stolen paintings. My real name is Bailey Rivers."

Silvie tilted her head slightly to one side. "So you're a detective and you don't want to be Amish?" Silvie pushed her fingertips to her forehead. "I can't believe what you're saying."

Bailey nodded. "I'm interested in becoming Amish now, but at the start I admit I was deceiving everyone. Elsa-May and Ettie are my grandfather's sisters. He left the Amish when he was fourteen and had no contact with his *familye* for a good twenty years after that. It was Elsa-May who persuaded the bishop to let me in to do my job."

Silvie pulled her hand away from his. "So that's how you did a *gut* job in your lies, you knew all the right things to say from your Amish relations. You didn't need to act so keen to be Amish. I've been deceived"

"Please don't be like that Silvie. It was my job."

Silvie turned her body away from his. "You should get another job." *I can't let him see me with tears in my eyes*, she thought.

He stood up and sat down on her other side. "Don't cry, Silvie, or you'll break my heart."

Silvie cried more at his words. "Would you ever join us?"

"I would, I think I would, only being a detective is part of who I am, a big part of who I am. I can't be Amish and a detective."

"It's just a job, Bailey. A job shouldn't define who you are," Silvie turned her face away from him once more.

"I can't explain it to you, Silvie. I'm sorry." Bailey put his hand gently on Silvie's cheek and turned her head to face him. "Silvie, what if I come back and join the Amish, for real?"

Silvie sniffed a couple of times. "You'd do that?"

Bailey stared intently into her eyes. "I'm seriously thinking on it, but I have to find the stolen paintings first. I can't let them get the better of me."

"How long will that take?"

He dropped his eyes from hers. "It's taken me nine years already."

"How close are you?"

Bailey shook his head keeping his gaze to the floor. "I headed down a wrong path thinking that Frank or his father had stolen some paintings. Now, I'll have to back track and pick up the trail again."

Silvie rose to her feet. "I hope you come back, but for now, it would be better if you left."

"I understand." Bailey stood up, walked toward the door and then turned around. "I'll always be thinking of you, Silvie."

"Don't say anything, Bailey. Just go." Silvie turned her back until she heard Bailey shut her front door. She turned around to check that he had gone then all strength left her legs and she sank to the floor. As tears came to her eyes, she knew that her *mudder* was right about love. It was all too *hatt,* and she was better off without it. Why hadn't she listened to her *mudder*?

Chapter 12

*For if a man know not how to rule his own house,
how shall he take care of the church of God?*
1 Timothy 3:5

As the widows sat around munching cookies, Maureen said, "I knew Bob wouldn't have been involved in anything bad. Besides, he didn't even need the money that Frank left him."

"*Jah*, he seems to be doing quite well for himself," Emma said.

Silvie and Ettie giggled.

"What are you two laughing at?" Maureen asked.

"We think you're growing fond of Bob," Ettie said.

"I've found out this week that there's more to Bob than we know. Just because he's quiet and doesn't speak to anyone people think that he's simple. He's not simple; it's just that when he doesn't have anything to say, he doesn't speak."

Elsa-May said, "I know a few people who could learn from him."

The widows laughed. They all knew a few folk in the community who liked to gossip a little too much.

Maureen said, "What about you, Silvie? What about Bailey?"

Silvie shrugged her shoulders. "I haven't heard from him."

Maureen put her hand on Silvie's shoulder. "*Ach*, it's only been a week, Silvie. I'm sure you'll hear from him. I know he likes you."

Silvie clenched her jaw. "Love's too much pain. I'm better off without it."

"Nonsense," Elsa-May said in her usual booming voice. "Love is precious and if you find it, you need to treasure it. It's just like a plant; starts with the seed, you cover it with the warm earth, water it and look after it."

Emma thought on Elsa-May's words. Maybe listening to Wil prattle on about his silly inventions would be the same as watering the seed. Emma knew she showed her love by cooking the things that he liked, but maybe she could do other things like listen to him and pay attention when he spoke on things that mattered to him.

"What do you mean, Elsa-May?" Silvie said, "I'm hardly in a position to do anything. I just have to wait until he comes back to the community – if he ever comes back."

"Silvie's right, Elsa-May. She just has to wait and if he comes back, he does, and if he doesn't, then it was never meant to be and she has to forget him," Maureen said.

"Nonsense," Elsa-May said. "I think Silvie should

pay the man a little visit. Remind him what he's missing."

Silvie's hand flew to her mouth. "Really? Do you really think I should visit him?"

"Why not? I would," Elsa-May said.

Silvie swung around to face Emma. "What do you think, Emma?"

Emma wished she hadn't been put on the spot. If she agreed with Elsa-May and things went wrong, Silvie might blame her. On the other hand, things could go well and Bailey might come back and join the community. "I can't say. I'm sorry, Silvie. You just have to listen to your heart. Maybe forget all those things your *mudder* told you about love; she sounds as though she was a very unhappy woman."

"What do you say, Maureen?" Silvie asked.

"I think you should pray about it, then listen to *Gott's* promptings in your heart. It's your decision."

"*Nee*, I'm totally against you going out and throwing yourself at the *mann*," Ettie said with unusual decisiveness.

Elsa-May gave a little chuckle. "Only you can decide, Silvie."

Silvie nodded. "*Denke* for all your opinions. I'll pray about it and have a think on it."

Elsa-May clapped her hands. "Okay, back to

business. Lacey has been arrested for the murder of Frank."

Maureen interrupted. "What about Andrew. Was he charged with anything?"

"*Nee*, he wasn't. Bob is keeping old Frank's *haus* and he's going to rent it out."

"Maybe Sabrina might want to rent it from him." Silvie giggled.

"*Ach*, is your *schweschder* still visiting?" Maureen asked.

"*Jah*, I'm afraid so. I guess I don't mind a bit of company. She does talk about Wil a lot though." Silvie turned to Emma. "Is everything okay with you and Wil?"

Emma forced a smile. "*Jah*, everything is just perfect."

"When are you going to marry the man?" Ettie asked.

"It's not been long enough." Emma was referring to the fact that it had only been just over six months from the death of her husband, Levi.

"I'd marry him straight away. What if he starts looking around? You know what these young single girls are like," Ettie said.

All eyes were on Emma waiting for a reply. She licked her dry lips. "I just need to wait until it feels right."

"How did we get back on to love when we were speaking on the case?" Elsa-May asked.

"Sorry, Elsa-May. I think it was when Bailey's name was mentioned." Silvie responded.

Elsa-May shook her head. "The paintings were original and worth a great deal. Bob is most likely the wealthiest Amish man ever."

All eyes turned to Maureen.

"Why's everyone looking at me?" Maureen asked.

The widows giggled.

"I think I will visit Bailey," Silvie said.

"*Gut*," Elsa-May said while she reached for a chocolate fudge bar.

* * *

On Emma's way home, she passed Wil's *haus* and saw his lights still on. Wondering if she should speak to him, she pulled off the road and into his driveway. *Nee it's too late at night; it's not proper*, she decided. She was just about to turn her buggy around when Wil opened his front door.

"Emma?"

"*Jah,* Wil, it's me."

"It's late."

"I know, I was just returning from visiting."

Wil walked over to her buggy and stood at the door. "Emma, I was going to call and see you tomorrow. I'm sorry; I was too hard on you. I just wanted more of your attention. Maybe it's me who's the selfish one."

"Wil, I want to apologize to you for taking you for granted. I've been too wrapped up in myself. I've been a selfish, horrible person."

Wil smiled and pulled her toward him and held her tightly. "*Nee*, you haven't been. I've been mean because I just want to marry you and I'm impatient. It's me who needs to apologize to you. I'm sorry."

They both laughed. Emma knew she would have to take an interest in the things that mattered to Wil even if she had no interest in them herself. Wil was right; he did show an interest in her sewing and things that she did. Why was it so hard to be interested in his hobbies? "So, you have no interest in Sabrina?"

Wil pulled back from her a little. "Sabrina? Of course not; she's a child."

"She's marrying age, Wil."

"She's a child to me. Anyway, the only woman I see is you."

She rested her head on Wil's shoulder and he held her a little more tightly.

"We should marry soon."

Emma shut her eyes tightly. "*Jah*, we should."

*** The End ***
****

Other books in the '*Amish Secret Widows' Society:*
The Amish Widow: Book 1
Accused Book 3
Amish Regrets Book 4

You may also enjoy these books by Samantha Price
#1 BEST SELLING
'*Amish Twin Hearts'* series:

Trading Places: Book 1
Truth Be Told: Book 2
Finding Mary: Book 3
Worlds Apart: Book 4

Also by Samantha Price - **#1 BEST SELLING**
'*Amish Romance Secrets'* series:

A Simple Choice: Book 1
Annie's Faith: Book 2
A Small Secret: Book 3
Ephraim's Chance: Book 4
A Second Chance: Book 5

Also a **#1 BEST-SELLING series-**
'Amish Wedding Season' series by Samantha Price:

Impossible Love: Book 1
Love at First: Book 2
Faith's Love: Book 3
The Trials of Mrs. Fisher: Book 4
A Simple Change: Book 5

Short Stories by Samantha Price in the *'Single Amish Romance Short Stories'*:

The Other Road
The Englisher Girl
Amish Runaway Bride
Amish Love Interrupted

****

Connect with Samantha Price at:
samanthaprice333@gmail.com
http//twitter.com/AmishRomance

Made in the USA
San Bernardino, CA
30 November 2014